Staged
4 Murder

J.C. Eaton

KENSINGTON BOOKS
KENSINGTON PUBLISHING CORP.

http://www.kensingtonbooks.com

KENSINGTON BOOKS are published by

Kensington Publishing Corp.
119 West 40th Street
New York, NY 10018

All Kensington titles, imprints, and distributed lines are available at special quantity discounts for bulk purchases for sales promotion, premiums, fund-raising, educational, or institutional use.

Special book excerpts or customized printings can also be created to fit specific needs. For details, write or phone the office of the Kensington Sales Manager: Attn.: Sales Department. Kensington Publishing Corp., 119 West 40th Street, New York, NY 10018. Phone: 1-800-221-2647.

Kensington and the K logo Reg. U.S. Pat. & TM Off.

First Printing: July 2018
ISBN-13: 978-1-4967-0859-5
ISBN-10: 1-4967-0859-8

eISBN-13: 978-1-4967-0860-1
eISBN-10: 1-4967-0860-1

10 9 8 7 6 5 4 3 2 1

Printed in the United States of America

PRAISE FOR J.C. EATON

Staged 4 Murder

"An eclectic cast of entertaining characters that will keep you wondering whodunit!"—Nicole Leiren, *USA Today* bestselling author, Danger Cove Mysteries, Heroes of the Night Series

Ditched 4 Murder

"The wedding from hell embroils a bookkeeper with a talent for solving puzzles in several murder cases . . . A hoot."—*Kirkus Reviews*

"Sophie 'Phee' Kimball has a lot on her plate in this captivating whodunit, but this feisty, take-charge heroine is definitely up for the challenge. Fun characters, a touch of humor, and a great mystery, the perfect combination for a cozy."—Lena Gregory, author of the Bay Island Psychic Mysteries and the All-Day Breakfast Café Mysteries

Booked 4 Murder

"A thoroughly entertaining series debut, with enjoyable, yet realistic characters and enough plot twists—and dead ends— to appeal from beginning to end."—*Booklist*, starred review

"You'll chuckle all the way through this delightful romp through Sun City West, as Phee and her mother unravel the mystery behind the sudden deaths of several book club members. It's so cleverly written, you won't guess the perpetrators until the very end."—Mary Marks, award-winning author of the Quilting Mystery Series

"*Booked 4 Murder* is a witty adventure that will leave you laughing out loud. Join Phee as she tussles with her wily mother, a cursed book, and a host of feisty retirees in this entertaining and charming cozy."—Stephanie Blackmoore, author of the Wedding Planner Mystery Series

"*Booked 4 Murder*, set in an Arizona retirement community full of feisty seniors, is a fast-paced mystery with a mother/daughter pair of sleuths who will keep you laughing until the last page. It will also make you think twice before choosing your next book club selection—THE END might come sooner than you think . . ."—Kathleen Bridge, author of the Hamptons Home and Garden Mystery Series

Books by J.C. Eaton

The Sophie Kimball Mysteries

BOOKED 4 MURDER

DITCHED 4 MURDER

STAGED 4 MURDER

BOTCHED 4 MURDER
(available January 2019)

And from Lyrical Press:
The Wine Trail Mysteries

A RIESLING TO DIE

CHARDONNAYED TO REST
(available September 2018)

Published by Kensington Publishing Corporation

To community theater companies everywhere,
with a special thanks to the Dryden Footlighters
in Dryden, New York, and the Penn Yan Theater Company
in Penn Yan, New York, for letting us take center stage
once in a while. You gave us great memories.

ACKNOWLEDGMENTS

We thank our lucky stars for our incomparable "pit crew" who are always there to answer the call. From double checking our manuscripts to handling all of our computer crises, you've never shied away. A big shout out to: Beth Cornell, Larry Finkelstein, Gale Leach, Ellen Lynes, Susan Morrow, Susan Schwartz, and Suzanne Scher.

Without our amazing editor, Dawn Dowdle from Blue Ridge Literary Agency, and our phenomenal editor, Tara Gavin, at Kensington Publishing Corporation, none of this would ever have come to fruition. We are so honored and appreciative.

For our dear friend, Michaele Gardella McGrath, who left us way too soon, we never forgot those stories you told us about your mother's horrid mink stoles. Thanks for inspiring us.

And to the stellar Kensington staff, we applaud all you do for us! Karen Auerbach, Robin Cook, and Ross Plotkin, you're the best!

Chapter 1

The wet sponge that hung over the Valley of the Sun, sapping my energy and making my life a misery for the past three months, wrung itself dry and left by the end of September. Unfortunately, it was immediately replaced by something far more aggravating than monsoon weather—my mother's book club announcement. It came on a Saturday morning when I'd reluctantly agreed to have breakfast with the ladies from the Booked 4 Murder book club at their favorite meeting spot, Bagels 'N More, across the road from Sun City West. I arrived a few minutes late, only to find the regular crew talking over each other, in between bites of bagels and sips of coffee.

"Who took the blueberry shmear? It was right in front of me."

"It still is. Move the juice glasses."

"I hate orange juice with the pulp still in it."

"If it didn't have pulp, it'd be Tang."

Cecilia Flanagan was dressed in her usual white blouse, black sweater, black skirt, and black shoes.

Don't tell me she wasn't a nun in a former life. Shirley Johnson looked as impeccable as always, this time with a fancy teal top and matching earrings, not to mention teal nail polish that set off her ebony skin.

Judging from Lucinda Espinoza's outfit, I wasn't sure she realized they made wrinkle-free clothing. As for Myrna Mittleson and Louise Munson, they were both wearing floral tops and looked as if they had spent the last hour at the beauty parlor, unlike poor Lucinda, whose hair reminded me of an osprey's nest. Then there was my mother. The reddish blond and fuchsia streaks in her hair had been replaced with . . . well . . . I didn't even know how to describe it. The base color had been changed to a honey blond and the streaks were now brunette. Or a variation of brunette.

The only one missing was my Aunt Ina, and that was because she and her husband of four months were in Malta, presumably so my aunt could recuperate from the stress of moving into a new house.

"You look wonderful, Phee," Myrna announced as I took a seat. "I didn't think you'd ever agree to blond highlights."

My mother nodded in approval as she handed me a coffee cup. "None of us did. Then all of a sudden, Phee changed her mind."

It was true. It was a knee-jerk reaction to the fact my boss, Nate Williams, was adding a new investigator to his firm. An investigator that I'd had a secret crush on for years when I was working for the Mankato Minnesota Police Department in accounting.

"Um . . . gee, thanks. So, what's the big news? My mom said the club was making an announcement."

Cecilia leaned across the table, nearly knocking over the salt and pepper shakers.

"It's more than exciting. It's a dream come true for all of us."

Other than finding a discount bookstore, I couldn't imagine what she was talking about.

My mother jumped in. "What Cecilia is trying to say is we have a firsthand opportunity to participate in a murder, not just read about it."

"What? Participate? What are you saying? And keep your voices low."

"Not a real murder, Phee," Louise said. "A stage play. And not any stage play. It's Agatha Christie's *The Mousetrap*, and we've all decided to try out for the play or work backstage. Except for Shirley. She wants to be on the costume and makeup crews."

"Where? When?"

Louise let out a deep sigh. "The Sun City West Footlighters will be holding open auditions for the play this coming Monday and Tuesday. Since they've refurbished the Stardust Theater, they'll be able to use that stage instead of the old beat-up one in the Men's Club building. All of us are ecstatic. Especially since we're familiar with the play, being a murder and all, and we thought in lieu of reading a book for the month of October, we'd do the play."

I thought Louise was never going to come up for air, and I had to jump in quickly. "So . . . uh, just like that, you all decided to join the theater club?"

"Not the club, just the play," my mother explained. "The play is open to all of the residents in the Sun Cities. Imagine, Phee, in ten more years you could move to one of the Sun Cities, too. You'll be fifty-five."

I'd rather poke my eyes out with a fork.

"She could move sooner," Myrna said, "if she was to marry someone who is fifty-five or older."

"That's true," Lucinda chirped in. "There are lots of eligible men in our community."

I was certain Lucinda's definition meant the men were able to stand vertically and take food on their own. I tried not to shudder. Instead, I became defensive, and that was worse.

"Living in Vistancia is fine with me. It's a lovely multigenerational neighborhood. Lots of activities . . . friends . . . and it's close to my work."

Louise reached over and patted my hand. "Don't worry, dear. I'm sure the right man will come along. Don't make the mistake of getting a cat instead. First it's one cat, and then next thing you know, you've got eleven or more of them and no man wants to deal with that."

"Um . . . uh . . . I have no intention of getting a cat. Or anything with four legs. I don't even want a houseplant. I went through all of that when my daughter was growing up. Now she can have pets and plants in St. Cloud where she's teaching."

The women were still staring at me with their woeful faces. I had to change the subject and do it fast.

I jumped right back into the play. "So, do all of you seriously think you'll wind up getting cast for this production?"

My mother nodded first and waited while the rest of the ladies followed suit. "No one knows or understands murder the way we do. We've been reading murder mysteries and plays for ages. I'm sure the Footlighters will be thrilled to have us try out and join their crews."

Yeah, if they don't try to murder one of you first.

"Well, um . . . good luck, everyone. Too bad Aunt Ina won't be able to try out. Sounds like it's something right up her alley."

My mother all but dropped her bagel. "Hold your tongue. If we're lucky, she and your Uncle Louis will stay in Malta until the play is over. It's bad enough having her in the book club. Can you imagine what she'd be like on stage? Or worse yet, behind it? No, all of us are better off with my sister somewhere in the Mediterranean. That's where Malta is, isn't it? I always get it confused with the other one. Yalta. Anyway, leave well enough alone. Now then, where is that waitress? You need to order something, Phee."

The next forty-five minutes were spent discussing the play, the auditions, and the competition. It was ugly. Like all of the book club get-togethers, everyone spoke at once, with or without food in their mouth. I stopped trying to figure out who was saying what, and instead concentrated on my meal while they yammered away.

"Don't tell me that dreadful Miranda Lee from Bingo is going to insist on a lead role."

"Not if Eunice Berlmosler has any say about it."

"She's the publicity chair, not the director."

"Miranda?"

"No, she's the lady who brings in all those plastic trolls to Bingo."

"With the orange hair?"

"Miranda?"

"No, those trolls. Miranda's hair is more like a honey brunette. Perfectly styled. Like the shimmery dresses she wears. No Alfred Dunner for her. That's for sure."

"Hey, I wear Alfred Dunner."

"You're not Miranda."

"Oh."

"What about Eunice?"

"I don't know. What about her?"

"Do we know any of the men who will be trying out?"

"I'll bet anything Herb's going to show up with that pinochle crew of his. They seem to be in everything."

I leaned back, continuing to let the discussion waft over me until I got pulled in like some poor fly into a vacuum.

"You should attend the auditions, Phee. Go and keep your mother company." It was Cecilia. Out of nowhere. Insisting I show up for the Footlighters' tryouts.

"You can scope out the men, Phee. What a great opportunity."

Yep, it'll be right up there with cattle judging at the state fair.

In one motion, I slid the table an inch or so in front of me, stood up, and gave my best audition for the role of "getting the hell out of here." "Oh my gosh! Is it eleven-thirty already? I can't believe the time flew by so quickly. I've got to go. It was great seeing all of you. Good luck with the play. I'll be sure to buy a ticket. Call you later, Mom!"

As I raced to my car, I looked at the clear blue sky and wondered how long I'd have to wait until the next monsoon sponge made its return visit to the valley. Weather I could deal with. Book club ladies were another matter, and when they said they were going to participate in a murder, I didn't expect it to be a real one.

Chapter 2

I was applauding myself for delicately balancing two iced coffees and two toasted bagels from Quick Stop when the phone caught me off guard, and I nearly spilled everything onto my desk. It was Thursday morning, and Augusta, our part-time secretary, wouldn't be in for another hour or so.

"Nate! I'm back with your iced coffee," I shouted. "Got to grab the phone." The voice at the other end, although not totally unexpected, made me jump. At least I managed to get four words out first. "Good Morning, Williams Investigations."

"Is this the infamous Sophie Kimball, who'll stick bamboo shoots in our fingernails if we lose a receipt?"

"Marshall? I . . . um . . . didn't expect to hear your voice so soon."

"So soon? It's been what? Almost a year? How are you doing? Wait! You can tell me everything as soon as I get there."

"There? Here? You mean you're in Arizona?"

"Unless hell decided to bake Mankato, I'm in Arizona. I can't wait to see you and Nate. Talk about a dream retirement job. Anyway, I'm at baggage claim at Sky Harbor and should be at your office in an hour. Got directions from Nate, plus the rental car will come with GPS."

"Super. I'll let Nate know. We can't wait to see you, either." *And I'll personally strangle your buddy for not telling me you were arriving today.* "Keep cool."

"Keep cool?" That was how I ended the call? That was the best I could come up with? What was I going to do when I actually saw him face-to-face? I reached for the small mirror I had tucked in my desk and studied my hair. It was okay. The blond highlights hadn't suddenly faded, and I looked all right. Then I had second thoughts and quickly added some blush to my cheeks, in case I didn't have enough color from the sun. If that wasn't enough, I applied lip gloss and sat staring at the computer like a seventeen-year-old girl who was just invited to the prom by the captain of the football team.

Nate sauntered into my office and reached for his iced coffee. Black. No cream. No sugar. He'd barely gotten it to his lips when the words flew out of my mouth.

"That was Marshall Gregory. He's here. In Arizona. At the airport. Marshall Gregory."

"Uh-oh. I knew I forgot to tell you something. Well, it's not like we have to pick him up or anything. Guy's renting a car. He'll lease one or buy one as soon as he's settled. I wasn't expecting him until next week, but he was able to get everything taken care of in Mankato and didn't want to hang around. Damn, it's going to feel good having another investigator here. Oh, and before I forget one more thing, you got a message from your mother while you were at Quick Stop. Want me to read it? She insisted I write it down verbatim, and I wasn't about to argue with her. Remind me to increase Augusta's hours. That's what she gets paid to do."

"Huh? What? My mother?"

I was still thinking about Marshall, and making a quick mind flip to my mother's message-of-the-day wasn't something I relished. I squinted as if expecting the worst. "Might as well. I'm ready."

"Here goes, kiddo." Nate tried to keep a straight face, but it wasn't working. "And I quote, 'We decided to go out to the Cheesecake Factory and reward ourselves for surviving auditions on Tuesday. The only ones who were unscathed were Shirley and Lucinda because they're doing the costumes. That miserable Miranda Lee was there giving us all dirty looks. Paula Darren was with her. Louise insisted Paula gave her the evil eye. The cast list will be emailed to all of us by tomorrow. Call me.'"

"Wow. I, um . . ."

"Don't tell me. Your mother and her friends tried out for a play?"

"Oh yeah. And not just any play. Agatha Christie's *The Mousetrap*. And since those book club ladies live to read about murders, they couldn't pass up the opportunity to act in one."

"Okay. But what happens if they don't get the parts?"

"Then we shutter the windows, disconnect the Internet, pull the landline, and get the heck out of town. Seriously? It will be unbearable. You heard my mother. Another would-be starlet gave them dirty looks. This will never end until the last curtain call."

"When's that?"

"Um . . . December, I think. The first week in December."

"Think of the bright side, kiddo. If your mother

and her friends do get the roles, they'll leave you alone for the next two months."

The thought of a few peaceful months almost brought a smile to my face until I remembered Marshall Gregory was going to walk through our door in less than an hour. I'd had absolutely no warning or I would have worn something that showed off my figure a bit more than a plain top and beige capris. I was going to say something, but Nate would have shrugged it off. Besides, it was best he didn't know how I felt about the firm's newest hire.

"You're being optimistic," I said. "I've got the next two months to listen to ramblings about who forgot their lines, who forgot the props, and who should have gotten the parts if they went to anyone but the book club ladies. All I can say is thank God I don't live in Sun City West."

"Oh, yeah. Speaking of that, Marshall's going to be renting a place not far from you. Thought you'd want to know."

I must have given him a weird look because he quickly added, "In case you need to share a ride or something."

Because seeing him every day won't be enough. Now he has to live near me.

Augusta arrived as Nate was heading back into his office. He turned and shouted out, "The new investigator I hired should be here in an hour. I forgot to tell you and Phee he was coming today."

"Not a problem, Mr. Williams. His office is all set up—computer, phone line, everything. All he needs to do is stick a photo of his family on the desk and he'll be up and running."

"Augusta," I said, "he's single."

"Okay. Fine. He can get a dog and stick a photo of

it on his desk. I have a friend at the Arizona Humane Society, and she told me they got in the cutest litter of Rottweilers."

Nate looked at her and shook his head. "No Rottweilers! No dogs! Let him get settled first. Plus, I've got so much work lined up, he's not going to have time to deal with a dog. If you want to do something nice for the guy, get him a six-pack and a subscription to Netflix. He's got everything else. He's renting a furnished place."

Augusta waited until Nate was in his office before asking me what Marshall Gregory was like. She knew I'd had a crush on him, but had no idea how overboard I really was.

"He's adorable in a Mark Harmon sort of way and really smart. And hardworking, too. Oh, and did I tell you he's got a terrific sense of humor?"

"Hmm, you don't say. By the way, you should get that puppy dog look off your face before the guy walks in the door."

"That noticeable?"

"Yep."

I picked up where I'd left off with the billing, but it took me longer than usual. It seemed as if I was jumping up, looking in my mirror and pinching my cheeks at every sound in the outer office, expecting it to be him. I deliberately left my door open.

What I didn't expect was a phone call from Shirley Johnson. "Phee, honey, you're not going to believe this!"

Oh God, no! I don't even want to imagine . . .

"Your mother got cast in the play! There are only three women's parts, and she got one of them—Mrs. Boyle. Of course, Mrs. Boyle gets killed at the end of act one, but still . . . it's a terrific role. Listen, before you say anything, I'm calling because your mother doesn't know. The cast list hasn't been emailed yet, but I can tell you who was cast. The part of Giles Ralston is going to be played by—"

My head started to swim. Marshall Gregory was going to walk into the office at any minute, and I was on the phone listening to a cast list.

"Shirley, that's wonderful. Absolutely wonderful. I've really got to get back to work."

"Don't you want to know how I found out?"

"I . . . uh . . ."

"I made the cutest little cloche for Eunice Berlmosler, the publicity chair, and she couldn't keep her mouth shut. Made me promise not to tell anyone until the cast was notified. Since you don't live in Sun City West, I figured that wouldn't count, and I just had to call you. And more good news. Can you imagine? Myrna Mittleson got the part of Miss Casewell. Probably because Myrna's so tall and when she walks it's like a stampede. She used to be really slow moving, but then she started those power move classes. Oh my, I'm going on and on . . ."

Suddenly, voices drifted in from the main office and I froze. Marshall!

"Myrna. Stampede. Power moves. That's terrific news, Shirley. Terrific. Thank you so much for calling. I've got to run. Talk to you soon."

Before she could answer, I placed the phone back in the receiver and leaned into my computer monitor, trying to look calm and nonchalant. The door to my office was flung open, and Marshall walked in, followed by Nate. Both of them had wide, silly grins on their faces. I stood as Marshall took a step toward me and gave me a hug.

"If this keeps up, we'll have the whole Mankato

Police Department working here. How're you doing, Phee? You look fantastic."

Even after a six-hour flight, he smelled as if he had just gotten out of the shower. I could detect a faint aroma of crisp apples (his aftershave maybe?), but it was over in a flash. Nate started talking, the phone began to ring, and a second later, Augusta announced in a voice that would put a longshoreman to shame, "Phee, it's your mother on the phone, and she says it's important."

"We'll leave you to your call," Nate said as he and Marshall headed out of my office. "I'm sure Marshall's starving, so how about if the three of us grab a bite at the deli when you get off the phone? Augusta can hold down the fort. I'm sure you're dying to catch up on the latest scuttlebutt from back home."

"Sounds good. Give me five minutes tops."

"I know your mother, kiddo. You can have ten."

I figured somehow, someone spilled the beans about my mother getting the part of Mrs. Boyle, and she was calling to let me know.

"Mom, is this about the play? Because if it is—"

"No. Why? What have you heard about the play?"

"Why should I hear anything about the play?"

Technically, I wasn't lying, but, so help me, if Shirley were to tell my mother I knew about this and I kept my mouth shut, I'd never be forgiven.

"Mom, why are you calling me at work? Is everything okay?"

"No. It's not. Something awful just happened. Myrna and I were having our nails done at that new salon next to the supermarket and when we got out to our cars, we both had the same threatening note on our windshields. A printed note. Not handwritten. Myrna wanted to call the sheriff, but I said no. I told her we'd call you instead, and maybe your boss can do something about it. We're next door to the salon, having coffee in that donut place. Myrna's at the counter, picking out donuts."

"Mom, it was probably an advertisement. What did it say?"

"It said, in bold print, 'AND THEN THERE WERE NONE.' You know what that means, don't you?"

"Yes. A new exterminating company is opening up in Sun City West. Did the note have any pictures of scorpions or bugs?"

"Don't be ridiculous. It was no exterminating company. Not like the last time when we found that horrid advertisement on my door. No, Phee, this was a threat. A threat right out of Agatha Christie's own library. Imagine! Using a title from one of her plays to insinuate Myrna and I are going to be killed, one at a time, like the characters in *And Then There Were None*. Someone didn't want us to try out for the play. I bet it was that miserable Miranda Lee."

I don't know why this popped out of my mouth, but I managed to make things worse. "If they wanted to threaten you and Myrna, they would have put a mousetrap with some cheese on your windshields."

"Sophie Vera Kimball, that isn't funny. Now, are you going to ask your boss to look into this, or do I have to tell Myrna to go ahead and call the sheriff's department?"

"No, don't call the sheriff. Whatever you do, do not call the sheriff. Look, I'll stop by your house on my way home tonight and pick up the notes. Nate and Marshall can look them over tomorrow."

"Marshall? The new investigator from back in

Mankato? I thought you said he wasn't starting until next week. Is he—?"

I lowered my voice to barely a whisper. "Yes, he's single, and he arrived early. Talk to you tonight, Mom. And tell Myrna not to worry."

Chapter 3

I didn't have to be a detective to figure out the note was written on plain white paper in a Times New Roman font. It could have been printed from anyone's computer, a fact that did *not* put my mother's mind at ease when I stopped by her house that evening after work.

"What are you saying, Phee? Anyone could have done this? Have them check for fingerprints."

"First of all, Mom, you're going to be hard-pressed to prove it was a crime. Second, the only prints we can be sure of are yours, Myrna's, and mine. And third, Nate hired Marshall because the workload keeps multiplying. From paying clients. But okay, okay, I'll show them the notes tomorrow. I've got to get going."

"You can't just walk out of here without picking up Streetman and giving him kisses. He expects that."

"Um, I think he wants food. He's standing next to the refrigerator pawing at it."

"Oh, you're right. It must be six-thirty already. That's when he gets his evening meatballs."

"You feed the dog meatballs?"

"Don't be ridiculous. I mix his dog food with a tiny

bit of shredded cheese and sometimes some crumbled hardboiled eggs. He gets three little meatball snacks at night."

I tried not to groan. My mother's chiweenie was probably the most doted on dog in the Greater Phoenix area. "Um, maybe you should feed him. I'll let you know what Nate and Marshall have to say about those notes tomorrow."

"Call me immediately if you think I need to worry."

"You won't need me to call you for that."

Nate's reaction when he read the notes the next morning came as no surprise. He laughed. "Not something I'd lose sleep over. Probably an off-beat ad or someone's idea of a bad joke."

"That's what I thought."

My boss and I were the only ones in the office, and I didn't want to appear too anxious about Marshall's whereabouts. I tried to sound matter-of-fact, but the words flew out of my mouth. "Is Marshall coming in today?"

"Nah. Thought we'd give the guy a break. He's getting his rental set up, unpacking, and presumably shopping for groceries or maybe just a case of beer and some pretzels. He also needs to transfer his driver's license to an Arizona one. Other than waiting in a long line, that should be a cinch."

"So, uh . . . when does he start?"

"He'll be in Monday morning. I've given him tons of paperwork to look over so he can jump into a few cases right away. He'll also need to get acquainted with the area. You know, roads, highways. The guy's an easy study, and the fact Phoenix is set up on a giant grid with only one diagonal street makes it real easy.

Listen, getting back to that note of your mother's . . . tell her and her friends not to get all worked up over it. I know how easy it is for them to jump to conclusions. It's probably a prank of sorts. It would be a different thing if the note was personalized, but this looks like amateur hour to me."

"I'm sure by now everyone in her book club has heard about it, so don't be surprised if you get a call."

By midday, I had all but forgotten about the note. That was when my mother phoned with the latest news about the play. She must have figured that since I had a lunch hour, it would be perfectly fine for her to take up most of it.

"I got the part, Phee! I got the part! The email came from Ellowina Bice. She's the director. I got the part, Phee! Oh, I said that already, didn't I? Anyhow, I'm playing Mrs. Boyle. And not only that, Myrna got the part of Miss Casewell. Isn't that fabulous? I thought Cecilia and Louise would be disappointed they weren't cast, but it turns out Cecilia was petrified she'd get stage fright, and Louise really wanted to be in charge of the props, so both of them are going to be doing that."

"Whoa, slow down, Mom. Congratulations."

I was hoping that in all of the excitement she'd forgotten about that note, but who was I kidding? The woman had a memory like an elephant. And a penchant for turning good news into something ominous.

"I'd be lying if I said I wasn't thrilled, but, honestly, I'm a bit unnerved. Someone must have known ahead of time Myrna and I were going to be in that play. That's why we got those cryptic notes on our cars.

Everyone knows we go in for our mani-pedis on Thursday. We were most likely being stalked. What did your boss say?"

"Um . . . er . . . the same thing I did. Probably a promo of sorts or a prank, and not to worry about it."

"Well, I hope that horrid Miranda Lee got a note, too. Can you believe it? They cast her in the lead. She'll be playing Mollie Ralston. Do you want to hear the rest of the cast? Chuck Mitchenson from Cecilia's church is playing—"

"Mom, I really don't have time to hear the entire cast list. You can tell me later. I'm working. Or, at least, I'm supposed to be. I'm really happy you got the part. When do you start rehearsals?"

"Monday morning at eleven. For a read-through."

"Okay, and congratulate Myrna for me. Love you. Bye."

I quietly thanked Agatha Christie, believing that, for the next two months, my mother would be so occupied with her performance I'd be spared from the drama that seemed to engulf everyone in her neighborhood. Boy, I couldn't have been more wrong.

As soon as the cast and crew met for the first time, my mother felt it was her duty and obligation to keep me informed of every little detail, beginning with the first read-through of the play. It was over a week later and I had just gotten home from a nice evening swim at the condo pool. As soon as I heard the phone, I knew it was her. Unless I felt like listening to it ring all night long, I had no choice but to pick up the receiver.

"Phee! You're not going to believe this. We had ou

first read-through today and met the stage crew. You're never going to believe who's on it."

"You're right. I wouldn't have the slightest—"

"Herb Garrett's pinochle buddies—Bill, Wayne, Kenny, and Kevin. And, of course, Herb. Like a bunch of old maids in pants, the five of them couldn't stop yammering. Finally, Ellowina, that's the director, told them they needed to work backstage with the stage manager while the cast went through the script."

"I didn't know Herb was interested in stage plays."

"Herb loves to hear himself talk. On the street, on the stage . . . it doesn't matter as long as his lips are moving. He's also interested in stage lighting. Apparently he has some background with it. Don't ask. And, as for the other men, well . . . from what I hear, Kevin and Bill are retired electricians so that helps, and Wayne's been in construction. I think Kenny's just along for the ride, but what do I know?"

"That's all very interesting, Mom. I've got work tomorrow—"

"That's right. I almost forgot. How's the new investigator doing?"

"Great. Really great. Takes a load off of Nate, and Augusta is thrilled to be working longer hours."

"What about you?"

"I'm fine. I like working with this crew."

"Well, that's more than the rest of us in the cast can say about everyone. That Miranda Lee is insufferable. She's a misery to be around, and we've barely gotten started. She had all sorts of demands for Ellowina, so Ellowina told her, in no uncertain terms, that, as the director of the play, *she* gets to make the artistic deci-
not Miranda."

huh."

"And one more thing . . . Miranda had the audacity to insist on her own dressing room. Her own dressing room! Do you hear me?"

"I hear you. Her own dressing room."

"Honestly, I don't know how any of us are going to survive the next two months if this keeps up. I heard she had some sort of squabble with Richard Garson, the stage manager, but I'm not sure about what."

If ever anyone lived up to the expression "a glutton for punishment," it was me. Why I continued to fuel the fire, I'll never know. "Um . . . what about the other cast members? What are they like?"

"Of course, you know Myrna, and then there's Gordon Web from our neighborhood watch group. He's playing Giles Ralston. And let's see . . . Len Beckers is playing Mr. Paravicini. I think they cast him because he looks like a Mr. Paravicini, very distinguished. Regal-looking face, moustache and all. Oh, and they cast Stanley Krumpmeyer as Christopher Wren. Again, type casting. Chuck Mitchenson from Cecilia's church got the part of Major Metcalf, and Randolph Tilden Jr. is Detective Sergeant Trotter. Randolph's the only one who has real stage experience. Myrna told me he's a retired theater professor from some college back east."

It was mind boggling how she went on and on without stopping to catch a breath. And even more astonishing that I even listened. After all, what did I care who was selected to play the part of Giles Ralston or Christopher Wren?

"Terrific. Sounds like a terrific cast. Um . . . it's getting late, and I suppose you'll want to get to sleep."

"I'm wide awake. Don't you want to know about the rehearsal schedule?"

No more than I want to know about the President's daily schedule. "I . . . uh . . ."

"The schedule is broken up into blocks. Read-throughs, act one, and act two. This week, I have to be at practice every afternoon from one to four, except Thursday, which is a good thing since I get my nails done then, and Wednesday, from eleven to one. Myrna's schedule is the same, except she has rehearsal on Tuesday morning. I'll call you in a day or so. No sense you trying to call me. I'll probably be out."

"Okay. That sounds good. Enjoy your rehearsals."

"Maybe Miranda Lee will quit the play. *Then,* I'll be able to enjoy rehearsals."

After a phone call like that, most women my age would pour themselves a nice glass of wine. I opted for making a milkshake instead. Extra chocolate ice cream and extra syrup. I didn't even know Miranda Lee, and I wanted her to quit the play like nobody's business.

Chapter 4

Rehearsals had been going on for over a week, and I grew to expect the usual late-night phone call from my mother as she grumbled about Miranda Lee.

"And I'm not the only one, Phee," she said on Thursday night. "You should have been there to hear her and Bill get into it. Bill's in charge of the spotlights, and what do you know? Unbeknownst to the director, Miranda told Bill she wanted a spotlight on her at all times. Bill told her where she could stick that spotlight and . . . well, I don't have to tell you the rest. You can only imagine."

By the following week, the tension on the set had reached a breaking point, according to my mother and the book club ladies. I was invited to join them at the Homey Hut for dinner on a Wednesday evening and took them up on the invitation. The place wasn't far from work, and I thought it would be a good time to visit with my mother and not get stuck for hours. In retrospect, I should have gone straight home and zapped a frozen dinner in my microwave. Sitting at the table with Myrna, Cecilia, Lucinda, Shirley, and Louise was akin to swatting flies at a picnic. The questions came at me from all over the place, and I felt as if I had all I could do to dodge them.

It started with Shirley. "Heavens, what would you do, Phee, if someone told you they wouldn't wear any costume that wasn't handmade especially for them?"

"I . . . uh . . ."

"Exactly. Lordy, I didn't know what to say. Now, I do not, and, I repeat, do NOT have the time to hand sew her costumes. It's bad enough trying to run all over the place to find vintage British clothing that matches the era."

"Oh, please," Myrna broke in. "It's much worse for me. Much worse. Miranda is constantly making snide remarks about my acting, and whenever we happen to be near each other, she says, 'Paula Darren should have gotten that part, not you.' Tell me, Phee, how would you handle it?"

"I guess I would talk with the director and—"

"Forget the director!" Lucinda shouted. "Ellowina is too busy fighting her own battles with that witch."

"Honestly, ladies, I don't understand how one woman can be so intimidating," I said.

My mother gave me a nudge and leaned toward me. "Then come to one of our rehearsals, and you can see for yourself."

Before I could say anything, the strangest thing happened. Everyone seemed to get a text alert within seconds of each other.

I seized that opportunity to bite into my turkey salad, but no sooner did I swallow the mouthful when Louise spoke.

"It's from Ellowina's niece. She got our email addresses from the cast list. Ellowina's in the hospital. They think it's food poisoning."

My mother all but lurched from her seat. "I knew it! I knew it! It was just a matter of time. I'll bet you anything Miranda Lee found a way to poison Ellowina."

"The text said food poisoning, Mom. Ellowina probably ate some tainted salad or something. Besides, why on earth would a lead character try to poison the director?"

My mother used one of her classic lines. "How should I know how crazy people think?"

Lucinda tapped me on the arm and shook her head. "Your mother's right, Phee. Miranda and Ellowina have been at it all week. I've got to read what the rest of the message says."

I watched as the women slumped over the table, cell phones in hand, reading each and every word of the text. Lucinda was shaking her head, and Shirley kept muttering, "Oh Lordy, Lordy."

"So, now what?" I asked.

"Ellowina left word with Richard Garson, the stage manager, to have everyone come in and run their lines as usual. All of the crews are to keep working."

Myrna slapped the table so hard we all jumped. "My God! It'll be like Armageddon."

"Maybe it won't be that bad," I said. "I guess she doesn't plan on being in the hospital for very long."

Louise let out a deep groan. "That's what you think. They put you in for observation, and, next thing you know, you're there for a month."

As much as I hated to admit it, as things turned out, Louise was right. Ellowina was stuck in the hospital with possible salmonella poisoning, something that kept the Maricopa Health Department on high alert. The good news was that between bouts of nausea and vomiting, she had managed to find a replacement director—Cliff Edwards, a community theater director from Peoria who owed Ellowina a favor.

According to my mother, half the cast thought Ellowina would return as soon as the antibiotics kicked in, and the other half figured she was on her way to the grave. Either way, they continued on like seasoned troupers. At least that's what my mother said.

Then, a week later on a Tuesday afternoon, Ellowina's food poisoning slipped to second place when someone found a dead body. Nate was in Tucson on a case, and Marshall wasn't expected back from Phoenix for a few hours.

No one could reach a consensus on the series of events that eventually led up to that horrific moment when the body was discovered. I'm sure that must have been frustrating for the sheriff's department, but honestly, these were the same women who couldn't agree on what kind of dressing to put on a salad, and, as for Herb's buddies, well . . . I didn't suppose they were going to be much help either.

I had barely set foot in the office when Augusta broke the news.

"Phee! Your mother's been trying to reach you! She's at the play rehearsal and says it's important."

"Now what? Did someone criticize her acting?"

"No! They found a dead body on the catwalk. Dangling over the edge in front of a large spotlight."

"Oh my God! One of the men must have had a heart attack. Or maybe got an electrical shock."

I quickly dialed my mother's cell phone, but it went to voice mail.

"Augusta, I've got to get over there. Please let Marshall

know when he gets in. No telling how hysterical my mother and her friends are."

"Of course. If you need anything, call me."

"I will."

I expected a fire truck and an ambulance to be in front of the theater, but when I arrived, all I could see was a lineup of deputy sheriffs' cars and a crowd of people in the parking lot. I knew, in that split second, that I would need to pass myself off as someone other than Harriet Plunkett's daughter in order to get inside.

Reaching for my Williams Investigations business card, and hoping that the word "accountant" wouldn't be too visible, I ducked under the yellow tape and made my way to the stage door where a sheriff's deputy was standing guard.

"Pardon me, I work for Williams Investigations, and I received a call from one of the cast members regarding the unfortunate incident. If you don't mind, I'd like to have a word with her."

The deputy took a quick look at my card and a closer look at me. I must have appeared fairly innocuous because he didn't question me further and opened the door.

"Miss Kimball, is it?"

I nodded.

"Our department is questioning all of the people who were in the theater. Cast, crew, recreation staff . . . Everyone's seated down in front. You'll need to check in with Deputies Bowman and Ranston since this is a closed area for the time being. You'll find them in the front of the auditorium."

Whew. It's a "closed area" and not a crime scene. Not yet, anyway.

The last thing I wanted to do was "check in" with Deputies Bowman and Ranston. I hedged to the side of the auditorium and stayed as close to the wall as possible. The dim lighting, coupled with the fact that the deputies were off to the side talking with one of the men, made it easy for me to slip in unnoticed. At least for the first eight or nine steps.

At that moment, Louise Munson shifted in her seat, caught a glimpse of me and shouted, "Harriet! Isn't that your daughter?" If that wasn't enough to get everyone's attention, she added, "That's Phee, all right. It *is* your daughter. She's walking down the outside aisle. OVER HERE, PHEE!"

Unbelievable. Louise Munson, whom I considered to be the only one in the book club with a voice that didn't rival a medieval fishwife, certainly had me fooled. Her shout echoed across the auditorium, and everyone turned to look. Including Deputies Bowman and Ranston.

I quickly grabbed the nearest seat and slouched down. I was close enough to see that they were talking with a good-looking, middle-aged man, and, other than giving the auditorium a cursory glance, the deputies went back to their conversation.

"Don't say anything. I'm not supposed to be here," I whispered as I took the empty seat next to Myrna. "Can you switch places with my mother?"

I'd seen kindergarteners handle a task like that with more finesse than the ladies who were seated in the same row as my mother. At first my mother tried walking over their legs, but that got too difficult so she asked them to stand. It was still a tight fit. Finally, four people in her row had to step into the aisle in order for the seat exchange to take place.

My mother sat up in her seat and surveyed the auditorium. Bending her head down, as if that would help keep her voice low, she moved closer to me.

"Thank goodness you got here, Phee. Did you bring your boss? I don't see him anywhere."

"No. What's going on? Augusta said someone was found dead on the catwalk, and the deputy at the stage door said this was a closed area. What was he talking about?"

"A murder. A possible murder!"

"Psst!" It was Myrna, leaning across my mother. "They didn't say it was murder, Harriet, but we're not stupid. Why would they have closed the building and brought in two deputies to question us? It's a crime scene, all right. They're waiting to make it official."

"Mom! Myrna! What on earth is going on?"

"It was horrific. Simply horrific. I don't think I'll be able to get a night's sleep after this. I can still see her arm dangling over the catwalk and that teal tunic draped over it."

"Her? Who?"

My mother inhaled as if she was taking her last breath. "It was Miranda Lee. Dead. Dead on the catwalk. We didn't know it at first when we all came in for rehearsal. Then all of a sudden Bill shouted out, 'We got a body up here, and she ain't moving.' And that's when I knew, Phee. We were all in trouble. That note . . . she was the first one. And then there were none."

"Stop it, Mother. You're making things worse."

"Worse? How can they be worse than a dead body right over our heads? All right, granted, it was . . . and God shouldn't punish me for saying this . . . but it was that awful woman, but still and all . . . murdered? In cold blood? None of us will be able to sleep after this. None of us."

My mother continued to mutter and mumble about murder and cold blood. When Shirley tapped me from the other side of my seat, I nearly shrieked.

"Lordy, this is bad. Real bad. Everyone in this room had something against that woman. She should rest in peace and not have her sorry soul a-wandering in our sights . . . so we're all suspects. Lordy, I do *not* want to spend the night in a prison cell waiting for someone to bail me out. I only have three nephews, and they live in Louisiana."

"No one's going to lock you up, Shirley. I can pretty much guarantee it." *What the heck am I saying? I have no idea what those deputies are going to do.*

Lucinda, who was seated in the row in front of us, spun around and leaned over the seat, her eyes staring right at Shirley. "Bill said it looked as if she'd been strangled. Electrical cords were all over her. He said her face was blue and puffy and—"

Shirley moved her index finger to her lips. "Hush yourself, Lucinda. I do *not* want to hear about puffy, dead faces."

A loud voice cut into the conversation. It was Bowman or Ranston, announcing the next cast or crew member to be questioned. "Chuck Mitchenson. Please come to the front of the stage. Chuck Mitchenson."

In that instant, my mother came back to the land of the living, and the hungry. "You could have brought us something to eat, Phee. Donuts or coffee cakes. We're going to be here for hours."

"Next time you call the office, you'll have to be more specific with Augusta. How was I supposed to know you'd be hungry?"

"Next time I go to a play rehearsal and walk into a dead person on the rafters over my head, I'll be sure to put in a takeout order."

A slender woman seated in the row across from us was sobbing hysterically. Another woman walked over, gave her a tissue, and walked away.

"Mom, who's that lady crying her eyes out? She must have been really close friends with Miranda."

My mother glanced over and shook her head. "No, she'd never met Miranda until rehearsals. That's Sue Ellen Blair. She's new to Sun City West, but she'd rented a place in Sun City for a year or so when she moved here from Wisconsin."

"Um, thanks for the detailed vitae on Sue Ellen, but I don't get it. No one else is crying."

"She's Miranda's understudy. I overheard her telling Herb that everyone is going to think she had something to do with Miranda's death in order to get the part."

"That's the kind of stuff you see in the movies. I mean about the understudy killing off the lead character. No wonder that woman is really freaked out."

Then, without any warning whatsoever, a medium-built, redheaded woman charged over to my mother, shoving a piece of paper in her face. The print was large enough for me to see what it said.

"This looks like something *you* would do, Harriet!"

My mother snatched the paper and tossed it back at the woman.

"You're insane, Paula. I got that same note myself. And Myrna did, as well. On our cars. In front of the nail salon."

"Miranda showed me this note. Plastered on her golf cart. It's no secret you never liked her."

"Few people did!" Lucinda blurted out from the row in front of us. "And just because Harriet thought Miranda was bossy, rude, self-centered, and vain doesn't mean she had anything to do with that note." Then, turning so that her face was directly in front of my mother's, she added, "You didn't, Harriet, did you?"

"Of course not."

Paula made some sort of a groan and started to turn away when my mother stood.

"And unless you want to deal with my attorney regarding defamation of character, you need to keep your mouth shut, Paula, and wait to be interrogated like the rest of us."

"Piss on you, Harriet!"

"Don't get too comfortable, Paula. Looks like more deputy reinforcements are arriving."

I glanced over my shoulder and instinctively lowered myself farther into the seat. The man walking down the middle aisle and straight for Deputies Bowman and Ranston wasn't one of their reinforcements. It was Marshall Gregory, and I swore he put Cliff Robertson and William Holden to shame.

"That's no deputy, ladies," I whispered. "It's the new investigator from my office."

"Lordy, Phee. I don't know about you, but he can interrogate me all he wants."

"No one's getting interrogated. The deputies are simply asking questions." *Except perhaps for me. I might get interrogated for impersonating an investigator.*

Chapter 5

Rather than have Marshall ferret me out, I jumped from my seat, ran to the back of the auditorium and thundered down the center aisle until I was only a few feet from him. It was either that or try to squeeze through one of the empty aisles, which were notorious for having less leg room than a commercial airplane.

"Hold up! Wait a second."

Marshall spun around and stepped forward until we were close enough to talk to each other without shouting. "I figured you had to be in this crowd somewhere, Phee. When the deputy at the door told me the other investigator from my firm was already in the building, I knew it had to be you."

"I can explain. All I did was show him my card and—"

Even with the dim lighting, I could see the dimple on the left side of his face as he grinned. "Don't worry about it. Your secret's safe with me. Give me the lowdown. What's this about a dead body? Not one of your mother's friends, I hope."

"Augusta called you, didn't she? I'm sorry you had to rush here from Phoenix."

"She was concerned about you and your mother. Tell me . . . What am I walking into?"

"The lead actress in the play, Miranda Lee, who, incidentally, was despised by cast and crew alike, was found dead on the catwalk this morning. One of the electricians who was working on the lighting found her and told everyone she might have been strangled."

"Oh, that's terrific. Nothing like getting a qualified opinion from someone who has absolutely no training in forensics. Nothing is for sure until the medical examiner passes judgment."

"I know. The deputies appear to be taking statements, but, according to my mother, all of the cast and crew came into the building at about the same time. Then Bill, one of the guys working the lights, went up the catwalk to get set up, and that's when he discovered Miranda. Listen, if the sheriff's department says it was foul play, it couldn't have been one of the book club ladies. Honestly. None of them are comfortable with heights. In fact, I had to go over to Cecilia Flanagan's house once, as a favor to my mother, to change the lightbulb over the kitchen sink."

"Slow down. Slow down. No one's accusing anyone of anything yet. Why don't you go back and sit by your mother. I'm assuming that's where you were before I walked in. I'll have a word or two with the deputies, and then I'll be right over."

"Um . . . has Nate told you anything about my mother and her friends?"

"Nate? No. Only your mother's name. Harriet Plunkett."

"Good. Good. It's always good starting with a clean slate. Uh . . . er . . . what I'm trying to say is my mother and her friends tend to jump to conclusions quickly, and well . . . oh, what the heck! You'll find out soon enough."

Marshall gave me a pat on the shoulder and headed straight for Deputies Bowman and Ranston, who'd just asked Randolph Tilden Jr. to report to the stage area. I returned to the seat next to my mother and looked across the stage. Randolph Tilden Jr. was nowhere in sight. I watched Marshall shake hands with one of the deputies while my mother wasted no time scrutinizing the Mankato Police Department's latest retiree.

"You didn't tell me the new investigator was so good looking, Phee. What is he? Divorced? Widowed? Gay?"

"What? You don't stop for a second, do you, Mother? He's single. That's all I know."

"Single. Hmm . . . That could mean anything. Of course, if it's a choice between widowed and divorced, you're better off with divorced. Divorced men are ready to move on. Unless, of course, you're stuck with someone who has to pay alimony. He doesn't have to pay alimony, does he?"

"SHH! How should I know? I don't have his dating profile. He's not someone I met on Match.com. For goodness sakes, I work in the same office as he does. That's all."

"And Kate Middleton went to the same college as Prince William. You saw how that turned out."

"Fine. Starting tomorrow, I'll enroll at St. Andrews University."

In that instant, another announcement was made for Randolph Tilden Jr. and a new announcement for Len Beckers. A tall man seated in the third row stood and strode to the front of the auditorium as if he was about to take a bow.

Someone shouted, "Hey, Bill, looks like the crown prince himself is going to honor the authorities with his presence."

The room got quiet and we could hear every word Herb Garrett's pinochle buddies were saying.

"Aw, give him a break, Wayne."

"I'd like for someone to give us a break and get us the hell out of here. They're wasting their time talking to Len Beckers. He didn't kill her. He wouldn't dare get his clothes all crumpled up on the rafters."

"How do you know? Since when did you become the expert on murderers?"

"It ain't murder until those two deputies say it is. For all we know, that darned woman could have strangled herself on the electrical cords."

New voices added to the cacophony, and I lost track of who and what was being said until Myrna spoke.

"What I'd like to know," she said, "is what Miranda was doing up there to begin with."

"I heard that!" Bill added from a few rows over. "You want to know what she was doing up there? What wasn't she doing? Meddling woman was on that catwalk more times than a lineman up a pole during a power outage. Always wanting the spotlight to be on her."

"How did Miranda know where she'd be on stage for that spotlight?" I kept my voice soft and low so that only my mother would hear me, or so I thought.

"I heard that, too!" Bill shouted. This time louder than before. "Why don't you walk over here so we don't have to twist our necks to speak?"

In that instant, one of the deputies stood and faced the cast and crew. "I'll ask you to please keep your voices down. Don't make this process longer than it has to be."

My mother bent her head down and motioned for me to do the same. "Blocking."

"Huh?"

"Blocking. It's the positions on the stage. Ellowina used a technique called triangular blocking. It centers on three pinpoints, so Miranda knew exactly where the spotlight should go."

"Oh. I see."

I was satisfied with my mother's answer, but for some reason she felt the need to continue. "The new director, Cliff Edwards, was changing some of the blocking and that really got Miranda in a tizzy."

"Why? Why should that matter?"

"Because she wasn't always center stage."

Lucinda spun around in her seat again, anxious to add her own commentary. "If you thought the arguments between Ellowina and Miranda were bad, you should have seen the ones between Miranda and Cliff. It was like watching Elizabeth Taylor and Richard Burton in *Who's Afraid of Virginia Woolf?*"

Myrna cleared her throat and whispered, "Everyone said she slapped him backstage during one of their fights."

"Who's everyone? I never said that, Myrna."

"Well, maybe not *you,* Lucinda, but everyone else."

I looked up to see Len Beckers returning to his seat and Marshall heading toward ours. Randolph Tilden Jr. was still AWOL. The next announcement was for Shirley Johnson.

She stood and edged her way toward us, her knees knocking into everyone in the row. "Oh Lordy, that's me. They want to question me next. Lordy, Lordy! What do I do now?"

I grabbed her by the elbow just as her knee hit

mine. "Just tell them the truth, Shirley. That you don't know anything."

"I might know something. Lordy."

"What do you mean?"

"The body . . . her body . . . she was wearing my teal tunic."

If this was a bad situation to begin with, I had the uneasy feeling that it was about to get worse.

"What do you mean she was wearing your tunic? Was it something from your personal wardrobe or something from the show?"

"It was mine. I kept it backstage to throw on when the air-conditioning got too cold. It was with the costumes."

"So someone who wasn't familiar with the play could have thought it was one of the costumes?"

"Heavens. I suppose so. But everyone on the set, except for maybe those cranky old men who work the lights, knows the play takes place in the nineteen fifties. In England. And no one would be sporting a teal tunic with a beaded fringe. I know I certainly won't be wearing it ever again, that is . . . *if* they give it back to me. I'm not letting my skin touch anything that was last worn by a dead person."

No sooner did Shirley say "dead person" when she collided into Marshall in the aisle and jumped back, nearly falling on top of my mother and me, since the "musical chairs" from earlier had put us close to the aisle.

Marshall reached over to steady poor Shirley and nodded at all of us. "Pardon me. Didn't mean to give you a scare. I'm Marshall Gregory. I'm a private investigator in Phee's office."

"I'm sorry," I said. "I should have introduced you

when Marshall first came in, but he needed to speak with the deputies."

A mumbled chorus of "nice to meet you" and "who?" was interrupted by another announcement for Randolph Tilden Jr. and one for Shirley.

"Lordy, that's me. I'd best be speaking to those deputies." She skirted around Marshall and walked down the side aisle.

"Excuse me a moment," Marshall said. "I need to have a word with Phee."

When we were out of earshot, he shook his head and groaned. "I've never seen anything like this in my life, and, believe me, I've been through lots of investigations. They don't even know if this Tilden guy even showed up for rehearsal today. And that's not the worst. How can they expect to get honest statements from everyone if people are allowed to sit here and talk with each other? Someone's bound to change their story if they think they have to protect a friend. Holy cow! I'm glad this isn't one of my cases."

"What did the deputies tell you? Do they think it's foul play?"

"It might be. Too early to say. They don't think it's a suicide, but it could be accidental. All they're trying to do right now is to get a statement from everyone who was in the building at the time the body was discovered."

"And then what?"

"They're going to be making an announcement after they question everyone. The theater is going to be closed for a few days while their investigation takes place."

"After that?"

"Then the show goes on, I suppose. They said they

have no intention of stopping the regular activities in this community."

"Don't they realize one of the cast or crew members could be a killer?"

"They do. In Bowman's own words, 'It's pretty darn likely someone in this audience knocked off the lead in the play, but hell, we can't keep everyone locked in here indefinitely while we investigate.'"

"So they're just going to let a killer loose in the theater?"

"In the theater . . . in the community . . . Until they know who did it, the cast and crew are presumed innocent."

"Maybe the director will cancel the play."

"Not likely. He told the deputies he planned to call the next rehearsal as soon as they get the all clear to be in the building."

"They may get the all clear, but that doesn't mean the cast and crew will come back. You heard Shirley Johnson. She's totally freaked out that a piece of her clothing was found on the dead woman. What do you think she and the other ladies are going to be like when they think there's a murderer in the room?"

"They may not have a choice."

"Huh? What are you saying?"

"Bowman and Ranston will need to keep a close eye on the cast and crew if indeed one of them turns out to be a killer. They need the play to go on. Bowman said they intend to have a sheriff's deputy in the theater at all times once rehearsals resume."

"Oh brother. That lucky stiff is going to earn his or her keep. It's funny, but my mother's friends are all shaken up over this, yet the men seem so . . . so . . ."

"Impervious?"

"Yeah, I suppose that's a good way of putting it."

"Got news for you. They're kind of unhinged, too, but they won't show it. According to the deputies, some of those guys would be downing a good stiff drink if they could get their hands on one."

"Did the deputies give you an idea of how long their questioning was going to take?"

"Maybe another hour or so. Did you want to stay and give your mother moral support?"

"You're kidding, right? I need to get back to work. And I'm really sorry for messing up your day. Things are under control around here. No reason for me to stay. I'll let my mother know, but I guarantee one thing."

"What's that?"

"She'll insist I stop by her house on my way home from work, so I'm doomed one way or the other."

"Doomed or not, are you hungry? Because I'm famished. What do you say we find the nearest restaurant?"

"Fine. But whatever you do, don't say anything about eating or we'll get stuck bringing them a take-out order."

Chapter 6

Even in the shadowy dusk, I recognized the lineup in front of my mother's house—Buick, Buick, Toyota, and Chevy. Had the book club ladies been there since the afternoon's "interrogation," or had they arrived recently? It didn't matter. Five minutes or five hours, I knew they were perseverating over the fact Miranda Lee was found dead. What I didn't know was whether or not they had ordered out or unearthed something from my mother's freezer.

No sooner did I pull up behind one of the Buicks when I got my answer. Hungry Howard's pizza delivery truck double parked, and the guy got out carrying four large pies. We both made it to the door at the same time. My mother motioned us inside.

Behind me, I heard someone shouting, "Hold that door, Harriet! I'm on my way in."

It was Herb Garrett, no doubt anxious to take part in my mother's impromptu rumor fest.

"Hey, cutie, how's it going? Did you drive straight here from work?" He followed me into the living room. "Here's my five bucks toward the pizza. Who's collecting the money?"

"Louise is," someone shouted. "Harriet already paid the delivery guy and gave him a tip."

Once the stack of pizzas was placed on the kitchen table, the guy bolted out of there. My mother had placed paper plates and napkins on the counter, along with bottled water and a few cans of soda. The dog came out from under the table and sniffed.

"Help yourself, everyone. No sense being formal. Sit wherever you want. And don't give Streetman any pizza with pepperoni or sausage. He gets gas. He can have plain cheese pizza. Oh, and don't give him the one with mushrooms either. I'm not sure if dogs can eat mushrooms."

Then, she turned to me. "You're staying for pizza, right? We ordered plenty."

"Thanks, Mom. Hi, ladies!"

While Herb and the women began to put pizza slices on their plates and find a place to sit, I spoke to my mother at the entrance to her patio. "I'm afraid to ask. How did it go? The questioning, I mean."

"How do you think it went? It was grueling. First, we had to give those deputies our name, address, and phone number. Oh, and our email address, too. I was waiting for one of them to ask for my blood type."

"That's pretty normal procedure. Then what?"

"Well, they wanted to know what time we got there, who we saw, who we spoke to, and where we were at the exact moment when Bill spied the dead body on the catwalk."

"Is that all?"

"No. They also wanted to know if any of us were in the building last night. After hours. Like any of us would be stupid enough to go into an empty theater at night. Even if it was open, which it sometimes is, because people forget to lock up. Anyway, the pizza's going to get cold. There are three kinds, plus cheese. Lucinda wanted plain cheese since she's on a diet."

I looked over at the women, who were either already eating or still piling pizza onto their plates. "Maybe Lucinda should stick to only two pieces of pizza if she's trying to lose weight."

My mother poked me. "Shh. She's right over there."

I seriously doubted anyone could hear me over the voices in the next room. As usual, the crew was all talking at once.

"Oh, and one more thing, Phee, before you go in there. We made a list for you."

I all but choked. "A list? What kind of list?" It would never be anything as normal as a shopping list because my mother and her friends wouldn't dare leave those decisions to anyone else.

"A list of the people you should talk to about Miranda's murder. You know . . . the suspects."

"The WHAT? The SUSPECTS?"

"Shh. Keep your voice down. They'll hear you."

"Let them. To begin with, no one knows if Miranda was killed or if it was an accident. But okay, okay. Let's just say, for argument's sake, she was murdered. I, of all people, am not an investigator. Why do you think the sheriff's department was questioning the cast and crew? I'll tell you why. Because they're the professionals who are conducting the investigation, not your daughter, the accountant."

"Accountant *and* bookkeeper. You have two certifications. Who better to conduct it than you? And before you answer, listen to me. You were the one who routed out the killers from the book curse last year. And what about my sister's master chef? You figured out who murdered him, too. Plus, you have a good way with people. They trust you. They open up to you. You think they're going to share their secrets with Deputy Bowman and the other one?"

"It doesn't matter. It's not my job."

"Let me ask you this. Why was that nice Marshall Gregory at the theater if your office isn't going to get involved?"

"He came to make sure you were all right. As a favor to me. That's all. Our office isn't taking the case. It belongs to the Maricopa County Sheriff's Department."

"They have enough to worry about . . . kidnappings, illegal aliens, drugs, guns . . ."

"Good. Now they can add mysterious death to the list."

"Harriet! We're out of napkins. If you tell me where they are, I can put them on the counter." It was Louise Munson, loud and clear from the kitchen.

"I'll be right there, Louise," my mother shouted as she gave me a nudge toward the pizza. "Hurry up before Herb eats it all. We'll talk about the list later."

The conversation in my mother's living room never wavered from Miranda's death. It included, but wasn't limited to: murders in Sun City West, the time it takes for a corpse to decompose, killers who were never apprehended, famous people who died under mysterious circumstances, and the best techniques for self-defense.

To prove the point that no killer was going to get past her, Shirley opened up her bag and produced a small aerosol can of bug repellent. "I'm too darned old for that self-defense hooey. That's why I carry a spray can of bug killer with me."

Lucinda snatched it from Shirley's hand and gave

it a once over. "That's fine if your killer is a mosquito or a gnat. What's this supposed to do if you get attacked?"

"I spray it in their eyes, step out of my heels, and run. I can still get around. What do you think, Herb? You're a man. Wouldn't this stop you?"

"What does my being a man have anything to do with this? And no, though it might annoy me. And it might really set off a deranged murderer."

"Is that what we have? A deranged murderer in our cast or crew! Oh Lordy! Harriet! Where's that list? Phee, you need to pay attention."

I chewed the crust from my pepperoni pizza slice and took a swallow of water. Like it or not, "the list" was going to be delivered to me as if it was a court-ordered mandate. I decided to sit quietly and continue to eat pizza while my mother spewed out a series of names, locations, and unrelated information that she and the ladies had somehow deemed vital to their cause. I lost count after the first three names.

"Stanley Krumpmeyer, broadcasting club, meets at seven AM in the men's club building on Meeker Boulevard."

"Gordon Web, has a small orange Pomeranian. Probably frequents the small dog park. Check with Cindy Dolton."

"Chuck Mitchenson, goes to Cecilia's church . . ."

Two slices of pizza and one bottled water later, I'd heard the entire list. Heard it. Not processed it. The women were looking at me as if they expected a categorical response to each of the names. Instead, I shook my head. "I'll be happy to deliver that to the sheriff's department on my way home."

Herb stood, reached for another piece of pizza and laughed. "They don't want the sheriff's department, cutie. They want you to poke around and see what you can find."

"For the zillionth time, I'm not an—"

"Yeah, yeah, yeah. Big deal. You work for one. Or is it two, now? Seems like a slam dunk to me."

My mother wasn't about to have Herb Garrett get the last word. "You're not getting off so easy yourself, Herb. How long have you been playing cards with those men? A year? Three years? How much do you really know about them? If I were you, I'd be asking a little more than who has the next piece of meld!"

Herb started to say something, but my mother cut him off and turned back to me.

"If you haven't noticed, Phee, all of us are petrified. I, for one, don't want to be looking over my shoulder when I'm squeezing fruit at the supermarket or wondering if someone broke into my car and is lying on the backseat waiting to put a choke hold on my neck. If we wait for those deputies to figure out who killed Miranda, one of us could be face down on the catwalk draped in Shirley's latest tunic."

At the word "tunic," Shirley gasped. "God help me! Don't you be saying that, Harriet."

"Calm down. I need to get my point across to my daughter. All we're asking, Phee, is for you to poke around in your free time and . . . well . . . you know . . . talk with people, figure out who had a motive. Obviously someone had the opportunity, or Miranda would still be alive bossing everyone around. And as for means? I don't really know what that is so don't worry about it."

I was all but screaming at this point. "We don't even know if she was murdered. She might have been the clumsiest person to go up on that catwalk. Why don't we wait until we know for sure?"

Shirley gasped again. This time louder. "Heavens! If I look up in that theater and see one of my beautiful pieces of clothing clinging to another dead body, I swear I don't know what I'll do."

I got up from my chair, took the list from my mother, and muttered six regrettable words before heading home for the night. "I'll see what I can do."

Chapter 7

"Does she think I'm certifiable or what?" I asked.

It was the next morning, and I was adamant Marshall needed to see the list my mother and her friends had prepared for me. Augusta was on the phone with a client, but I intended to show her the names once she was done with the call. I thrust the paper in front of Marshall before he could say anything.

"Look at this note! Would you look at this note? It says 'You'll find Cindy Dolton at the dog park every morning at six. Plenty of time to get the lowdown on Gordon Web before you have to be at work.' At six in the morning all I want to do is have a cup of coffee. Oh my gosh. You must think I'm an awful whiner."

"Nah. I know you better, and I also know you'll probably wind up tracking down some of your mother's so-called suspects because you won't want to disappoint her."

"Marshall, I—"

"Hey, I understand. That group of women in the book club may be a bit eccentric, but they've got a right to be alarmed. From what those deputies told me yesterday, the first responders were all but placing bets it was murder."

"So you think I should take this list seriously and start asking around?"

"Only if you stick to high profile places with plenty of visibility, and if anything makes you feel the least bit uneasy, get the heck out."

"My God! Now you're sounding like my mother. Next thing I know you'll be reusing paper plates."

"Whoa. That was unfair."

I figured it was time to change the subject, so I asked about Nate. "Any idea when he'll be back from Tucson?"

"Maybe the end of the week. Meanwhile, I've got to get a jump on my next case. I'll catch you later today."

Today was Wednesday. I had no intention of throwing myself into another one of my mother's wild goose chases, especially one in which the goose could have my neck. Still, having a conversation with Cindy Dolton in the dog park wasn't that onerous. I figured I'd get up early the next day and get it over with.

Cindy was the owner of a small white dog named Bundles and an acquaintance of my mother's. I'd met her over a year ago when rumors of a book curse circulated around the community. She knew just about everyone in the dog park, so if there was anything at all remotely suspicious about Gordon Web, Cindy would be able to tell me.

As it turned out, it wasn't until Friday that I had the chance to catch up with her. I was swamped at work with invoices and the monthly billing. Having a second investigator, even one I couldn't seem to keep my eyes off of, meant more work for me. I had to double check on his direct deposit, make sure our health insurance company added him, and verify his employment with the company that handled our business insurance. Little things, but time consuming when continuously placed on hold.

My mother called me the night before Cindy and I spoke to let me know the new director, Cliff Edwards, had arranged for a full cast read-through on Saturday at the social hall. No crew. Only the cast. Apparently, he didn't want anyone to forget their lines, and he certainly didn't want to lose the momentum.

"Do you have any idea when they'll let you back into the Stardust Theater, Mom?"

"According to Cliff, who spoke with the sheriff's department, we should have the all clear by Tuesday."

"That's good, I suppose. I mean, all things considered, you didn't lose too much time."

"Oh, we lost time all right, and now it'll mean longer rehearsals since the calendar was already in place. It would have been awful if the Footlighters had to change the date. Too many conflicts with other performances."

"Other performances? You mean to tell me there's more than one play going on?"

For a brief second, I wondered if someone was trying to sabotage the play and it went too far.

"No. Performances. The square dancers, the yodeling club, the Jazzy Tappers—"

"I get it. I get it. Spare me the entire list."

"Speaking of lists, did you get started? Did you talk to Cindy? What did you find out about Gordon?"

"Nothing yet. I'll see Cindy tomorrow morning if I can keep my eyelids open."

"Cindy knows more people than just the ones from

the dog park. Read her the entire list and see what she has to say."

Yes, that's exactly what I intend to do at six in the morning. "Uh-huh."

"Cecilia intends to sprinkle holy water in the theater when they open it back up for us. Can you imagine?"

"If that makes her feel better, Mom, then what's the harm?"

"Because the next thing you know, Shirley will be armed with an arsenal of Lysol and she'll be spraying *that* all over."

"Good grief. Miranda Lee was probably strangled or electrocuted from the wiring. She didn't die of the Bubonic Plague."

"Shirley doesn't believe in taking chances."

"What about you? Are you okay with it? Going back inside the theater, I mean?"

"Of course not. For all I know I could be sitting next to the murderer. That's why the book club ladies and I came up with the buddy system."

"Buddy system? Like in summer camp?"

"Exactly. No one goes anywhere in that building alone. I don't care if it means changing seats to another row during rehearsal or using the restroom. We go in pairs or we don't go at all. Cliff Edwards will have to deal with it."

"Yeah, I suppose he will."

"Call me, Phee, if you find out anything."

"Same here. And stop worrying. Whoever murdered Miranda, and I'm not saying she *was* murdered, but *if* she was, then whoever did it had a motive."

As soon as I got off the phone, I felt guilty for telling a white lie. Even though I did it so my mother wouldn't worry. Like those high-strung book club women, I had the same creepy feeling that maybe we *were* dealing with a serial killer, and maybe the note, "AND THEN THERE WERE NONE," was his or her way of getting the real show started.

Like clockwork, Cindy was at the dog park Friday morning at six. I was sitting under the yellow awning holding a cup of Dunkin' Donuts Dark Roast. The misters were on full blast because the three ladies sitting next to me insisted they'd pass out if there was no moisture in the air.

The second Bundles came through the gate, I got up and headed straight for Cindy.

"Hi! Good Morning! I'm not sure if you remember me, but I'm Harriet Plunkett's daughter, Phee."

"Oh no. Not another book curse?"

"No. Nothing like that. Murder. Um . . . possibly murder. I'm not really sure."

Cindy was about to say something to me when all of a sudden she whipped her head the other way and yelled, "Get away from that black and white dog, Bundles! Now! Mommy said NOW!"

Then she turned back to me. "That black and white terrier pees on the other dogs. Two nights ago he came sniffing around my Bundles and next thing you know, he peed all over him. I had to rush home and give poor Bundles a bath. Let me tell you, I was not happy. Not at all. Uh . . . what was it you were saying? Something about murder?"

"I can't say for certain it was murder. But one of the cast members in the Footlighters' play was found dead in the theater a few days ago."

"Miranda Lee, right? You couldn't get within five feet of her table at Bingo. I knew it had to be something suspicious. I just knew it. Everyone was keeping it hush-hush like she had a heart attack or stroke or something. In fact, it was in this morning's paper, but all it said was that a deceased person was found in the Stardust Theater. Heck, I gloss over that stuff all the time. Gee, you think she was murdered? Harriet thinks she was murdered?"

"Let's put it this way, the sheriff's deputies are investigating, but my mother doesn't want to take any chances, what with her being in the play and all. She asked me to see what I could find out about the other cast and crew members and thought you might know one of them."

"Oh my God! A real killer could be in that play. Or in this dog park! Near my Bundles! Who? Who does she think it is?"

"She doesn't. She and her book club friends made up a list of names. Here, see for yourself."

I took the list out of my bag and handed it to Cindy. Her gaze went up and down the paper as if it were the menu from Cracker Barrel.

"Hmm . . . I know three of these people. Gordon Web has a purebred, orange Pomeranian named Creamsicle Boy, Bill Sanders has a scruffy, tan-and-white mutt named Kramer, and Miranda Lee used to own a Chinese Crested Hairless dog that went by the name of Lady Lee. That was at least four years ago. The poor dog was on its last legs then."

"Do you know if Miranda had any problems with Gordon or Bill?"

Cindy tried not to laugh, but she couldn't help it. "Bill gave her a wide berth and Gordon wouldn't give her the time of day. Other than bringing their dogs to the park, they had nothing to do with each other. I really don't think either of those men could be your killer. I mean, why wait all this time to murder someone? Miranda was as obnoxious four years ago as she was four days ago."

"Um. It's a possible murder. Possible. Her body was found on the catwalk above the stage. She could have tripped on something and gotten tangled up in the cords."

Cindy shook her head. "Miranda didn't trip. I could all but guarantee it. Miranda Lee was a former nurse. They're trained to be steady on their feet. Especially if they're carrying syringes or tubes or any of that stuff."

"How do you know that? About her being a nurse?"

"Sweetie, you'd be surprised what we learn by sitting here in the dog park. The dogs may be wagging their tails, but their owners are wagging their mouths. Listen, if I hear anything, I'll call your mother."

I thanked her and started for the gate just as I heard someone yell, "POOP ALERT! POOP ALERT BY THE WATER FOUNTAIN!"

I ducked out of there before someone decided to hand me a clean-up bag. It was six-thirty, and that meant I'd get to the office two hours early. Two hours that I desperately needed to catch up. It felt as if I was constantly being pulled away with my mother's phone calls, not to mention the entire half day I lost when Miranda's body was discovered.

Marshall had left a message saying he would be in Phoenix, and Nate was still working in Tucson. I had the entire place to myself and was able to send out invoices without feeling rushed and reconcile some accounts without hurrying through them.

Augusta arrived at nine. The second she walked through the door, she headed straight for my office.

"I think Marshall likes you, Phee. And I don't mean in the everyday sense of the word."

"Whoa! What brought that on? And do you really think so? Because that would really complicate matters. On the one hand, I'd love to be dating him, but, on the other, if things don't work out, it would be really awkward around here. Really awkward. My God, Augusta. I just used the word 'really' four times. I'm worse than a fourteen-year-old. I'm even speaking like one."

"You're even blushing like one. No use worrying about it. See what happens. If it's meant to work out, it will. Well? How did your encounter at the dog park go?"

"Let's put it this way, the Federal Bureau of Investigation agents are amateurs in the intelligence business compared to the folks who hang out there. If Miranda Lee really was murdered, the dog park people will know about it way before the authorities."

"Then what?"

"Then we'll all have to hide from my mother."

Chapter 8

It was back to routine the following week. That meant work for me and taking advantage of the last days of the late summer weather by going swimming at night. I had made a few friends in my community and having a social life meant more than eating at Bagels 'N More with my mother's book club ladies.

As far as the play was concerned, the cast and crew returned to the Stardust Theater and picked up where they left off, with a few exceptions—Sue Ellen Blair was now playing the role of Mollie Ralston, a sheriff's deputy was in the building for all rehearsals, and my mother's new protocol of being with a buddy at all times was put into effect immediately. I imagined she'd nagged the new director into it until he acquiesced.

Four days went by without a hitch. Then the deputy on duty delivered the official news to the cast and crew. He made it clear Miranda Lee's death was ruled a homicide. It was one in the afternoon, and I was in the middle of printing out a spreadsheet when Augusta poked her head in my office.

"Your mother's on the line, Phee. She's yelling, 'It

was murder! It was murder!' I think you'd better take this call."

I picked up the receiver and took a breath. "Hi, Mom, Augusta told me—"

"We knew it! We knew it all along, Phee. None of us are safe. The only way we'll be safe is if we know for sure it was a designated murder."

"A designated murder? You mean like a designated driver? What *do* you mean?"

"I mean a single, premeditated murder meant to murder one person and one person only, not some lunatic out to bump off the entire cast and crew. We can only pray that the culprit wanted to knock off Miranda Lee, and only Miranda Lee. How are you coming along with that list I gave you? Have you narrowed down the suspects?"

"Um . . . well . . . I'm working on it."

"What have you found out so far?"

It was a good thing I was on the phone and not talking face-to-face with my mother. She'd see me biting my lip, and she'd know I wasn't exactly tackling her list in a timely fashion. Or any fashion for that matter.

"Cindy Dolton gave me some information. I'm looking into it."

"Well, keep looking. And while you're at it, you might try talking to Sue Ellen Blair. It would look suspicious if one of us started grilling her."

"It's going to look even more suspicious if, out of the blue, someone who has absolutely nothing to do with the play suddenly starts pumping her for information."

"It's not out of the blue. You're with an investigative agency. You can slip into one of the rehearsals and ask her a few pivotal questions."

"Don't tell me. You've written those down as well as the list. Look, I'm sure if there are any *pivotal* questions to be asked, the deputies have already done so."

"Not the kind of questions *I* have. I want to know that woman's theatrical ambitions. She may have been bawling her eyes out on the day of the murder, but all that tells me is Sue Ellen Blair might be a better actress than any of us could imagine. Maybe she wanted the role of Mollie Ralston so badly she was willing to murder for it."

"Dear God, Mother. This is community theater, not Broadway."

"Exactly. If it was Broadway, they'd hire a hitman. This is a retirement community. People don't have money for that sort of thing. All the more reason why you need to take that list seriously. At least when we thought there was a possibility Miranda's death could be accidental, we were able to function. But now . . . now it'll be like walking the London streets with Jack the Ripper on the loose."

Short of banging myself in the head with the phone receiver, I couldn't see any easy way out of this conversation without fabricating some sort of interruption. "Nate's at the door, Mom. I've got to get back to work."

"Call me when you get home. If I'm still alive at the end of today's rehearsal."

"And you thought Sue Ellen was dramatic? You'll be alive, Mother."

I took the spreadsheet from the copier and filed it. Nate liked having a hard copy of all the financials as well as the cyber version. In some ways, he was more like my mother's generation than mine. Maybe it was the twenty year age difference and the fact that old habits, such as needing written tangible evidence, died hard. Then something dawned on me.

Tangible evidence. Had the sheriff's deputies uncovered anything on the catwalk that would link back to the killer? If so, they weren't about to share that information with the cast. But maybe the men who worked the lights would have noticed something out of the ordinary. Especially Bill Sanders, who found the body. I grabbed my calendar and jotted down "Bill, dog park, Kramer." A quick call to Cindy Dolton and I'd have that mutt's potty schedule down pat. And hopefully, the dog was an evening pooper.

My mother had calmed down considerably by the time I called her later that night. She and Myrna had been "glued at the hip" from the minute they entered the Stardust Theater. Myrna had also purchased a small device called "The Screamer" for her keychain. If anyone tried to attack her, one push of the button and a deafening scream would reverberate throughout the building. The device, or Myrna's own shriek.

To placate my mother, I decided to really tackle "the list." I figured I'd begin my "inquest" with Bill Sanders the next evening after work. According to Cindy Dolton, Kramer was a regular fixture at the dog park between five-thirty and six-thirty and had made a habit of tipping over the water bowls.

"You'll be able to spot that dog right away, Phee. He goes straight to the community bowls, sticks his paws in them, and dumps the water."

"What about Bill? How will I recognize him, other than his being tall? I didn't get a good look at him in the theater. The lighting was dim, and I wasn't really paying attention." *And some of those old men look alike.*

"He'll probably be wearing a dark blue baseball cap. If not, he's bald on top but has lots of wild, curly hair on the sides. Looks like Larry David, only older. More than likely, you'll hear him first."

"What do you mean?"

"Oh, inevitably some dog will do something that upsets Bill, and he'll get on a rant. Huffing, puffing, and stomping all over the place."

I was grateful for Cindy's information because it took me less than three minutes at the park gate to locate Kramer and his master. I could hear the commotion across the parking lot.

"That's not a community watering bowl. It's Kramer's own bowl. His special park bowl. And that basset hound just took a drink from it and got specks of dirt in the water. I've got to pick them out before Kramer will drink from the bowl!"

Stepping into the park, I asked a tall, blond lady why they couldn't simply refill the water bowl from the hose.

"You must be new here. Bill brings bottled water for Kramer. Not the cheap kind, either. The expensive Geyser Spring Water."

I smiled and thanked her. Geyser Spring Water for a dog. It made me question my own parenting skills, since the only water my daughter drank when she was growing up came from the tap.

Bill was sitting on one of the benches under the palm trees and painstakingly removing bits of debris from the water bowl. I immediately took the seat next to him and said hello.

He looked up. "Can you believe this? A million water

bowls and none of those dogs can leave Kramer's bowl alone. Which one is yours?"

"Oh, I don't have a dog. I stopped by in case one of my friends was here, but I don't see her. She's working on that play for the Footlighters and was really upset about the news."

"There's more news? What news?"

"The cast and crew found out one of the actors was murdered."

"Oh, *that*. I could have told you that on day one, seeing as I found the body."

"You did? How awful! How horrible for you."

"Eh. More horrible for her. Miranda Lee, that is. The body. Sprawled out on the catwalk with all those cords all over her. Looked like she strangled herself, but there was something fishy. Looked like someone stuck that tunic over her after she was dead."

"What do you mean?"

"It looked staged. The way the electrical cord was around her neck and her arm dangling. Now I'm not saying she wasn't strangled or maybe even electrocuted, but whoever did it wanted it to look like it was an accident. Accidents ain't that neat."

"Um . . . yeah. I suppose."

"And there's another thing. When Kevin and I, he's another electrician on the crew, finish up for the day, there are no cords lying around. It's a regular safety hazard on a stage, but on a catwalk, it's a disaster. If you ask me, someone wanted it to look like we were the ones responsible. Now, don't get me wrong, I'm not happy that they said it was murder, but if it was an accident, it would be my butt and Kevin's they'd be coming after."

A thought raced through my mind. Was someone devious enough to commit murder and make it look as if Bill and Kevin were at fault? Nah, no one could be that diabolical. I muttered, "Uh-huh," as Bill continued to talk.

"You know what the worst thing was about that Miranda Lee? Excluding her personality, of course, which was none too pleasant. I'll tell you what. It was her perfume. That sickeningly sweet, flowery perfume that got into my nostrils every single time she climbed up to the catwalk to mess with the lighting. I'm not saying I'm pleased she bit the dust, so to speak, but it's a damn good relief not to smell that perfume anymore. That stuff lingers, too. Worse than an old fart."

I stifled a laugh. "Was there anything else odd about the scene of her death?"

"Odd how?"

"I don't know. Maybe something out of place. Other than the electrical cords."

Bill scrunched up his mouth until it touched the bottom of his nose.

"Perfume smelled worse. Pungent. Maybe it gets that way on a dead body, but, come to think of it, there was a crumpled up instrument schedule a few feet from Miranda's head. I figured it was probably an older version that Kevin meant to throw out. No big deal."

"What's an instrument schedule?"

"I guess you're not too familiar with play productions, huh? It's a spreadsheet that lists every fixture in the show and every detail. Before we had spreadsheets, it was written on grid paper."

"What happened to that instrument schedule?"

"I don't know. Probably got thrown out."

"Tell me, other than you or Kevin, who would need an instrument schedule?"

"Oh heck, lady, lots of people. The director, for

one. Then the stage manager, the assistant stage
manager, and anyone on the lighting crew. Oh hell! I
bet I know where that darn instrument schedule came
from. I bet Miranda had it all along. That woman
was always on the catwalk trying to readjust the pipe
clamps."

It was like having a conversation with an auto
mechanic. I was totally lost. "Pipe clamps?"

"Yeah. They attach the fixture to a hanging position. She wanted the fixtures spaced so she'd get
'optimum exposure.' Her words. Not mine. Well, guess
she got her wish, huh?"

I nodded as Bill went on and on about stage lighting.

Finally, I broke in. "From what I've heard, she
wasn't too well liked."

"Got that right. Say, you look familiar. Have we met
before?"

"Um, er . . . Not exactly. I'm Harriet Plunkett's
daughter. Phee."

Suddenly Bill stood and started yelling. "Kramer!
Kramer! You get your nose out of that dog's butt!"

I took that as my cue to get going and quickly
thanked Bill. "It's been nice chatting with you. I'll
make it a point to see the play."

Closing the gate behind me, I wondered if that
instrument schedule had inadvertently dropped from
the killer's pocket as he or she struggled with Miranda,
or if Miranda had had it all along. Either way, it was
one clue that was now missing.

Chapter 9

"Don't bother about Sue Ellen Blair. It couldn't possibly be her."

No hello. No "Good morning, did I wake you?" No greeting. Those were the only words out of my mother's mouth so early in the morning that my alarm clock hadn't even gone off. It took me a good thirty or more seconds to register what she was saying. Let alone what day it was—Friday.

"Huh? Wha—?"

"I thought you'd be up by now, Phce. I was going to call you last night, but it was so late when we got back from rehearsal. The schedule's been completely changed, so we go day by day. Different days. Different scenes. Who the heck knows what that director is going to do. Not like Ellowina. She was much better organized."

"Uh-huh."

I fumbled for my reading glasses as I cradled the phone against my ear.

"Well, like I was saying, you don't have to question Sue Ellen. I'm sure she had nothing to do with Miranda's murder."

By now I was awake enough to process the conversation. "Why do you say that?"

"Because Sue Ellen was nearly killed last night. It scared the daylights out of all of us."

"Killed? How?"

"She was on stage for one of the scenes and all of a sudden, *BOOM!* Out of nowhere. Fine, not exactly nowhere, but one of the lights from that strip of overhead lights came loose and crashed inches from her. Inches! Not feet. Inches. She's lucky she wasn't killed on the spot."

"You mean an entire lamp from the strip of lights? Which, by the way, is called a batten. I got an earful yesterday about stage lighting from Bill when I saw him in the dog park."

"Yes. That. The entire big black thing. It crashed to the ground. The lighting crew swore up and down they had fastened those clamps, but somehow one came loose. And I'll tell you another thing. They don't come loose by themselves. It's the murderer. Sue Ellen was so panicked, it took a full forty minutes for her to calm down and run the scene."

"I can imagine. I'd be pretty shaken up, too."

"Then, if that's not bad enough, the stage manager starts going on and on about the cost of another tungsten-halogen lamp. All the while Sue Ellen is bawling her eyes out."

"Yikes."

"So now, before we rehearse, Herb promised they'd lower that batten thing and check the clamps."

"Good idea."

"For the lights, maybe. But I'm telling you, Phee, it's the killer, and he or she isn't done yet. Maybe they won't get us with the lights, but it'll be something else. All of us are on edge. Anyway, you can cross Sue

Ellen off your list and question someone else. You *are* working on that list, aren't you?"

"Of course I am. I just told you I spoke with Bill Sanders last night at the dog park."

"Good. Good. What did you find out?"

"Not much. Except for one thing. He thought Miranda's body was staged, which would mean someone draped Shirley's tunic over the corpse."

"Whoever did it, had to have done it on that catwalk. It would have been near to impossible to drag a dead body up there."

"I agree with you, Mom. But why would they bother staging the body? Unless they were trying to hide something. But what? Dead is dead, don't you think?"

"I think that if you don't act fast, there'll be more dead bodies lying around, and I don't want mine to be one of them. As soon as you get out of work, go interview someone from the list. If I were you, and I'm not telling you what to do . . ."

Sure you're not.

"I'd start with Paula Darren. Find out all you can about Miranda Lee from her. If it's not a crazed serial killer, then it has to be someone with a darned good motive to kill Miranda and then go after the rest of us to make it look like a deranged psychopath. For your information, the news media is all about delusional murderers. It's as commonplace as road rage killers or those meth addicts who go berserk."

I'd been down this road before, and I knew I had to get off the phone before my mother dredged up every recent story from *48 Hours, 20/20,* and *Frontline.*

"Fine. Fine."

"I'll save you some time. There's no rehearsal tonight, and I guarantee you'll find Paula at Karaoke

Night in the Ocotillo Room at Beardsley Rec Center. It costs two dollars if you plan to sing."

"That's the last thing I plan to do."

"Call me when you find out something."

Suddenly my alarm clock went off, and I reached across the nightstand to shut it off. "That's my cue, Mom. I've got to get going."

"Remember, call me."

"As soon as I find out anything, I will. And if I don't find out anything, I'll still call. Probably tomorrow. Try to have a good day."

"I'll try to stay alive."

A loose clamp on a lighting batten probably wasn't that unusual, but, given the circumstances, I didn't blame my mother for her reaction. She was right about one thing, though, and that was trying to find a motive for Miranda Lee's murder.

Nate was still in Tucson, but Marshall had arrived in the office before I did.

"Good morning, Phee! How's the hunt for Red October going?"

"Very funny. It keeps getting worse by the minute."

I proceeded to tell him about the official ruling on Miranda's death and the near-death encounter Sue Ellen Blair had had at last night's rehearsal. I also filled him in on my conversation with Bill Sanders at the dog park.

"My mother is convinced the deputies are doing little to nothing and that the only chance of finding out who killed Miranda rests with my would-be investigative skills. Can you imagine that? I don't know where she gets those ideas."

"From what little I've heard, I'd say she was pretty astute. Besides, it doesn't do any harm probing into the matter as long as you don't overstep the actual investigation."

"So you think I should be doing this, too? Following that list of hers and talking to possible suspects?"

"I wouldn't expect any less from you. Just be careful."

"Well, tonight should be a whole lot of fun, then. I'm going to attend Sun City West karaoke at one of the rec centers. It's where Miranda Lee's good friend, Paula Darren, goes on Fridays, according to my mother."

"No play rehearsal tonight then?"

"Nope. There'll probably be an afternoon one on Saturday."

"Hmm, do you plan on belting out a song tonight or just jumping into questioning mode?"

"What? Me? Sing? Never. I'll simply find a way to approach Paula and hope I can get somewhere with her. She's really the only one who knows anything about Miranda."

"I've never gone to a karaoke night. Or anything karaoke for that matter."

I wasn't sure if he was hinting at an invitation or merely making a statement. He must have sensed my hesitation because he immediately caught himself.

"Yeah, work has totally consumed me in the past, so there are lots of entertainment venues I've never explored. Although casinos aren't really my thing, and I doubt I'd enjoy Bingo."

"I think you'd find Bingo to be a real eye-opener around these parts."

Just then Augusta walked through the door and

greeted us, saving me any further conversation with Marshall about entertainment options.

At the end of the day, all he said was, "Let me know how it goes tonight. Either way. Your singing or your sleuthing."

Karaoke Night in the Ocotillo Room began promptly at six-thirty. I arrived an hour later, having stopped at a local deli to grab dinner first. The music hit me as soon as I set foot in the Beardsley Recreation Center Building. A formidable lobby with floral chairs and tables opened into a long corridor that led to the assorted activity rooms, each named for a different species of cactus. The restrooms were straight ahead, marked with cowboy/cowgirl silhouettes.

It was easy to spot the Ocotillo Room. It was the only one that showed any signs of life. A few people were milling around the doorway and others were coming in or going out. I showed my visitor card to the man at the entrance, and he waved me inside without saying a word.

It took a minute or two for my eyes to adjust to the dim light. I suppose the organizers wanted the place to look more like a nightclub than an activity room for senior citizens. The large round tables with six to eight chairs were almost filled to capacity. Who knew this was such a popular pastime? In front of the room a man and a woman were singing Sonny and Cher's "I Got You Babe." They stood on a rectangular platform, each holding a wireless microphone.

In the back of the room, it looked as if soft beverages and snacks were being sold. Some of the tables had wine bottles on them as well as beer. I figured it had to be BYOB. I walked toward the refreshment table, turning my head so I could get a good look at the audience. Wherever Paula Darren was seated, I intended to be close by so that if she got up for refreshments or to use the ladies' room, I could somehow start a conversation with her.

Having seen Paula on two separate occasions, a year ago at Bingo and more recently at the Stardust Theater when she accused my mother of writing that bizarre note, I knew I'd recognize her. Not many women have red hair in a pageboy with straight bangs.

I leaned against the back wall and perused the tables again. It was tough to get a good look since so many backs were turned away from me. The couple on the platform finished their song and were enjoying the applause. A heavyset man thanked them and introduced the next singer, someone named Larry, who was about to sing Bobby Darin's classic, "Mack the Knife." I skirted past the refreshments until I reached the wall opposite the entrance. It gave me another vantage point to look for Paula. I was so intent on locating her that I didn't realize someone was speaking to me, and I was completely taken by surprise.

"Are you waiting for your turn?" a man whispered as he walked past me.

"My turn? What? Oh no. I'm not singing."

"You should. It's fun. My date and I were going to sing "You're the One That I Want" from *Grease,* but she's not back yet from the ladies' room and we're up next. Hey, want to pitch in and sing it with me? If we lose our spot, we won't get it back. It's a long sign-up list."

"I . . . uh . . . er . . . I can't sing."

"Can't or too scared?"

"Both, but mostly can't."

"Too bad. I wish Paula would have waited a few minutes. We'll miss our turn for sure."

"Paula? Your date's name is Paula?"

My Aunt Ina would have said something about the planets being lined up in all the right places, but I knew it was nothing more than coincidence. Coincidence if his Paula turned out to be the one I wanted to find. I took my chances.

"Paula Darren's your date?"

"How did you know? Do you know her?"

"In a manner of speaking. Um, maybe I can hurry her along for you. 'Mack the Knife' has at least six stanzas. Maybe more. I'll see what I can do."

Without waiting for a response, I took off for the ladies' room like no one's business and kept my fingers crossed Paula was still there.

Chapter 10

As I swung the ladies' room door open, I heard a voice. "Have they called the next number yet? 'You're The One That I Want'?"

"Not yet," I shouted as I stepped inside. Judging from the open stalls, Paula Darren was the only woman in there. She was standing in front of the mirrors fixing her hair.

She paused for a second to acknowledge me and continued with her hair. "I'm supposed to be singing that number, and it's the last thing I want to do. I told Barry, my date, that I don't like to sing in public, but he was chomping at the bit for us to perform. I can act, mind you, but sing? Only in the shower. I'll tell him it was really crowded in here and took longer than I thought. He'll believe me. He's seen some of those lines."

"Uh-huh."

I stood there wondering what to say next. I was sure if she got a good look at me she'd recognize me from that day in the theater. No sense pretending. I started to open my mouth when Paula continued.

"Do me a favor, would you? Can you go into the

hallway and listen to hear if they've moved to another
song? I don't want to take a chance if Barry's out
there."

"Sure."

At first I didn't hear anything, and then, like something out of a nightmare, I heard a voice that resem-
bled chalk on a blackboard. A woman had started to
sing "Total Eclipse of the Heart." Bonnie Tyler would
be pulling her hair out.

"I think you're okay, which is more than I can say
for the audience. They've moved on to another song.
One we should both miss."

"Yeah, sometimes it's really bad."

Paula had turned away from the mirror. "Say,
didn't I see you at the Stardust Theater? I did, didn't
I? You were sitting near Harriet Plunkett and her
friends. Are you on one of the crews?"

*She hasn't made the full connection. I'm safe for the time
being.* "Uh, actually, I'm with Williams Investigations
in Glendale. I was called to the theater when Miranda
Lee's body was discovered. Horrible thing. I'm sure
it's devastating for everyone involved in the play."

So far, so good. I haven't really lied yet.

"It's a nightmare. No. Worse than a nightmare.
People can wake up from nightmares. Poor Miranda
will never wake up."

"Did you know her well or only from the play?"

"Miranda and I were good friends. Really good
friends. We've known each other for over a decade.
I don't know why anyone would have wanted to kill
her. What have you found out? Are you working with
the Maricopa County Sheriff's Department?"

"My boss is. Working with them, that is. And no, no
information as of yet. You wouldn't happen to know
if anyone had anything against her, would you?"

"She didn't have any enemies, if that's what you mean. But, well, Miranda wasn't always the easiest person to get along with. Not that she was mean, spiteful, or vindictive, nothing like that . . . but she was kind of territorial when it came to her table at Bingo. And that sort of carried over into the play."

"What do you mean?"

"She didn't just walk on the stage; it was like she had to own it. Own it and be recognized."

"Recognized? She had the lead role."

"She wanted to be the focal point of attention in every scene. Went so far as to adjust those stupid spotlights herself. If only she could have let it go. She'd still be here. I know for a fact she had more than one argument with those grouchy old men on the lighting crew."

"Are you saying you think—"

"That one of them did it? No. She also got into it with both directors, Ellowina and Cliff. And my take is, there was something weird about her and Cliff, but I couldn't quite figure it out. He probably knew how to push her buttons, that's all. Once he accused her of negligence because she moved Randolph's skis, well, not Randolph's. The character he's playing. Sergeant Trotter. Anyway, Cliff claimed someone could have tripped over them and gotten seriously injured."

"It must not have been too pleasant around the set."

"It wasn't, but it wasn't all Miranda's fault, either. I really hope whoever killed her gets caught."

"Yes. Of course. That goes without saying. I'm very sorry for your loss. Ten years is a long time to have been friends with someone. Did you meet her here in Arizona?"

"Seemed like yesterday. We both bought our homes around the same time. We had a lot in common. I'm a retired ER nurse, and she was a floor nurse for a rehabilitation hospital in Phoenix. We were also both recently divorced, although Miranda never wanted to talk about that. Poor Miranda. We had a small memorial service for her. Just a few of her friends. She was cremated and the remains sent to her niece in Rhode Island. That's her only surviving relative, as far as I know. I imagine the niece will have the remains buried in Rhode Island since that's where Miranda was from. Oh my gosh. I've been in here forever. Barry is going to pitch a fit. I'd better get going."

"Well, it was nice talking with you. Good luck with the karaoke."

"Ugh."

Paula raced out the door as I stood in front of the mirror. Seconds later, two women dressed as if they had been working the rodeo circuit walked in. I said hello and made my exit. It was eight-forty when I started my car and headed back to Vistancia. I made a mental note to keep a low profile around my mother and her friends while they were at rehearsals, lest Paula discover the truth about me. And the fact Williams Investigations wasn't officially investigating.

When I got home, the red light was flashing on my phone. I pushed the button and waited for the message.

"Phee, we're having breakfast at Bagels 'N More tomorrow morning at ten. Cliff called a rehearsal for one-thirty. Shirley thinks Miranda's ghost is in the theater. Come to breakfast. Oh, I also left you a voice mail on your cell. Turn that thing back on, will you?"

Wonderful. A ghost. Miranda's ghost. That was the last thing I needed to think about before I went to sleep.

Since I didn't have anything major on my schedule

for Saturday morning, I decided to take my mother up on her offer and meet the Booked 4 Murder ladies at their regular spot. I figured if I could sift through the rumors, gossip, and innuendos, I might be able to hone in on something important pertaining to Miranda's death.

I could see the giant banner plastered across the building as I pulled into the packed parking lot the next morning. The sign read WELCOME BACK SNOW-BIRDS, and I groaned. It would be frenzy time in there, and I was right. Every table was full, and the waitresses seemed to be bouncing from one table to the next.

Somehow my mother had managed to commandeer the large table in the middle of the room for her group. All six of them, including her. I wove around the smaller tables until I finally arrived and took a seat next to Shirley, who was in the middle of a conversation with Lucinda.

"I don't like salty lox."

"Then don't order it."

"Hi, everyone," I said as I made myself comfortable and reached for a menu. "How's the play going, or shouldn't I ask?"

Shirley moved the menu away from her eyes and looked up. "Miranda's ghost is haunting the theater. Didn't your mother tell you about it?"

"Sort of. She left a general message on my phone last night."

"Well, I'll give you more than a general message. Let me tell you, that evil woman's spirit never left the Stardust Theater. She's not going to rest in her grave until the killer's found."

"Shirley's right," Cecilia said. "That theater needs

to be cleansed, and I don't mean spraying a bottle of Lysol everywhere."

I looked from face to face and they all seemed to concur with Cecilia. Well, almost all of them.

My mother was engrossed in studying the menu and only looked up once; she directed her comment to me. "Spit it out. What do you think?"

"Me? I don't even know what's going on. Why do you think the place is haunted all of a sudden?"

Before anyone could say a word, the waitress appeared and cleared her throat. "I know. I know. Separate checks. What's it going to be, ladies?"

I jumped right in, ordering bacon, egg, and cheese on a plain bagel, hoping everyone else would be as quick. They weren't. I fought hard not to bite my lip as the questions began.

"How fresh is the tuna salad?"

"How salty is the lox today?"

"Are they still putting egg in the potato salad?"

After what seemed like a millennium, the waitress took the orders and headed for the kitchen. At least we'd managed to keep it simple as far as coffees were concerned.

As I poured half-and-half into my cup, I went back to my original question. "What makes all of you think the place is haunted?"

Louise gave Shirley a poke in the arm and whispered, "Tell her."

"Fine, fine, Louise. I don't need any prompting. Three days ago I walked into the costume room and what did I find? Mollie Ralston's costume wadded up in the middle of the floor. That was the role Miranda was playing until . . . well, you know. Anyway, I had to iron that brown wool skirt and press the beige cardigan to get rid of the wrinkles. And the blouse. The white blouse was filthy. I had to throw it in the wash. Everyone else's costumes were still in the closet on hangers, where they should be."

"Um, did you ask Sue Ellen if she knew anything about it?"

"Of course. That was the first thing I did. Poor girl took one look at her costume on the floor and started crying."

"It doesn't sound like anything supernatural to me. Sounds like something a flesh and blood person did for some inane reason."

"That's not the only thing. You tell her, Myrna. You saw it. It happened during the act two rehearsal."

"What happened during act two?" my mother shouted. "How come no one told me? My character's not in act two. What did I miss?"

Myrna put both elbows on the table, clasped her hands, and put them under her chin before speaking.

"We were midway through act two when the lights started flickering. At first I didn't think anything about it since the guys are always adjusting them, but then, out of nowhere, this really weird shadow appeared in the projection booth. Cliff stopped the rehearsal to ask who was up there, but no one was. None of those lights should have been on because it wasn't a technical rehearsal. Cast only. The lighting crew wasn't even there that afternoon."

"Well, someone was there," I said. "And I'll wager anything it wasn't Miranda's ghost."

Louise reached across the table to grab another napkin. "There's other stuff, too, Phee. I've been going to plays and movies in that theater for years and the temperature is always the same. Lukewarm. Not anymore. Sometimes the blower comes on by itself and gusts of cold air are everywhere."

"Look, all of this has a logical explanation, I'm sure of it. Hasn't the director spoken with the maintenance department for the rec centers?"

Some of the women shrugged, while others shook their heads.

I was about to suggest someone call the maintenance department when something dawned on me. If the ladies were so preoccupied with the idea that Miranda's ghost was in the theater, then they wouldn't attribute the bizarre activities to something more sinister. It could very well be that the killer was doing those things to throw them off. But why? If all he or she wanted to do was kill Miranda Lee, then there was no need for this charade. Unless . . . oh my gosh! What if my mom was right and it was a serial killer?

"Phee! Phee! Move your arm out of the way. The waitress is trying to put the plates down."

I was so engrossed I hadn't noticed our food being served. My mother, however, was right on top of things, as usual. All conversation ceased as breakfast was being served. The women were eyeballing their plates with more scrutiny than the county food inspector. Then, without warning, they began a new conversation that reminded me of a television game show. "I should have ordered the—fill in the blank—instead."

Only a few words escaped their mouths amid the chomps, crunches, and chews.

We were almost done eating when my mother leaned back in her chair to stretch. "Look! There's Herb with Kevin. Maybe one of them can tell us what's going on with the lighting. We've got two extra seats at this table. Let's call them over."

The men were seated in the far left corner.

"Mother, do we have—"

Too late. My mother stood, waved her arm, and motioned for Herb to join us. Seconds later, the two men took seats at our table.

"Hey, gorgeous ladies! Good timing. We were just getting up from the table when we saw you. Looks like all of you have eaten, too. So, what's new?"

"You tell me, Herb," my mother said. "Aren't you the least bit worried about all the goings on at the theater? You know . . . the lights going on and off, the temperature, the shadow . . . the . . ."

I could tell Kevin was trying hard not to laugh, but it was impossible. "Electrical glitches, that's all. And as for the temperature fluctuations, that old thermostat probably needs to be recalibrated or replaced."

My mother wouldn't give up. "What about finding the Mollie Ralston costume piled up on the floor? That's no glitch. What about that, Kevin?"

The guy shrugged. "No, I'd say that was someone who was pissed off. Maybe sweet, little Sue Ellen Blair isn't as nice as everyone seems to think, and she rubbed someone the wrong way. Look, all of this crapola is just that—nonsense. But there's one thing that's really starting to get on my nerves, and when I figure out who's responsible, they're going to get an earful from me. Unless, of course, Bill gets to them first."

The look on my mother's face was priceless. She was dying to know the rest. "What are you talking about?"

"That stinkin' perfume Miranda Lee always wore. It's permeating the catwalks and making me gag."

Shirley just about swooned in her chair. "Lordy, oh

Lordy! I knew it. I knew it. Temperature fluctuations and calibrations my sweet patootie! It's Miranda Lee. Come back to haunt all of us until we can put her soul to rest."

At that moment, I waved my hand in the air and yelled, "Check, please!"

Chapter 11

While the waitress was busy doling out the checks, I took that opportunity to get everyone's attention.

"Hold on. Before any of you head out, did Randolph Tilden Jr. ever show up in the theater that day? The deputies kept calling his name, but he wasn't there."

I quickly turned to my mother and added, "Sorry, Mom. Forgot to ask you."

Myrna immediately responded with a loud "No," which was followed by a more detailed explanation from Cecilia, who apparently heard what had happened to Randolph from Chuck Mitchenson at church a week later.

"Randolph woke up with a terrible earache and had to go to one of those urgent care places. Forget your primary care doctor in an emergency. They're too busy to take you. Randolph told Chuck he left a message for the director, but I guess Cliff never got it. You know how it is with voice mail. You end up deleting half the stuff before you listen to it."

"I don't delete anything, Cecilia," Myrna said. "You must not know how to use your phone."

"Of course I know how to use my phone."

Another fifty seconds of listening to Myrna and Cecilia, and I'd swear I'd break out in hives. "Um, forget the phone. Did the deputies ever question Randolph?"

Cecilia couldn't wait to provide the specifics. "Not only did they question him, but, according to Chuck, they all but accosted him in front of his own house. There he was, picking up the Saturday evening paper in his driveway when a sheriff's deputy car pulled up. Imagine! Having to stand there and answer all sorts of questions in front of the entire neighborhood."

Myrna shook her head and mumbled something to the effect that "It couldn't have been that bad."

"Well," I said as I started to stand, "guess that pretty much sums up the missing Randolph Tilden Jr., huh?"

"Don't go running off, Phee!" It was my mother, and I tried not to cringe.

I wasn't about to get off the hook that easily with just a breakfast; she had to have something else in mind.

"I need to speak with you for a minute once we pay the checks. Meet me at the car when you're done."

I nodded, said good-bye to the ladies, as well as Herb and Kevin, and walked over to the cash register. Using a debit card made it a whole lot easier than the production that was still going on at the table.

The ladies' voices were anything but soft.

"Does anyone have three cents?"

"Who has change for a quarter? My tip should be one sixty-five, and I don't want to overpay."

"Do you count the tax in with the bill when you figure the tip?"

"Do you think someone's going to steal the money

we're leaving on the table? I hate leaving it right out in front."

As I finished up at the cash register, someone tapped me on the shoulder.

It was Louise Munson. "If I were you, I'd be looking into that Randolph Tilden Jr."

"What do you mean?"

"Oh, nothing specific, but did you ever meet someone who kind of gave you the willies, like there was something 'off' about them?"

"I don't know. Maybe."

"Randolph is one of those people. I picture him tearing the wings off of flies and saving them in numbered envelopes."

"Ugh. That's a horrible thought."

"Like I said, I don't know why, but he gives me the creeps. Keeps to himself a whole lot, too. Not like the other players. When they're on break, they're yacking to all of us on the crew. Not Randolph. Even when he walked into the prop room. He announced whatever he needed if it wasn't on stage and then left. Like that. After a while, I got used to it. Randolph would come in, say something like, 'notepad and pen,' and then head out the door."

"It sounds as if he's very businesslike, that's all. Mom told me he was a former theater professor back east."

"So I've heard. Someplace like Massachusetts or maybe Rhode Island. Or was it New Hampshire?"

"Did you notice any tension between him and Miranda?"

"Wherever Miranda went, there was tension. Of course, I was so busy with the props, still am, as a matter of fact, that I didn't notice anything with those two. Now, Stanley Krumpmeyer is an entirely different story."

"Huh?"

"He plays Christopher Wren. And let me tell you, there was no love lost between the two of them. I was on stage right, ready to replace the small wobbly stool with another one, while Miranda and Stanley were doing a scene together. She stopped dead in the middle of her lines and accused him of upstaging her."

"I imagine the director must have been furious."

"Oh, he was. He most certainly was. Told them both to take a five-minute break. Then he yelled for Miranda to speak with him in the back of the auditorium. What happened after that, I don't know. I switched the small tables on the stage and went about my business."

"Wow. Thanks, Louise. For sharing that. I'd better get going. Mom's waiting for me by her car, and she's probably wondering what's keeping me so long."

I walked as fast as I could, but it didn't make any difference.

My mother was as impatient as ever. "Goodness, Phee. What took you so long? If you would have paid cash, you could have left it on the table and gotten out of there."

"Louise wanted to tell me something about Randolph and Stanley."

"What? Does she think one of them killed Miranda? She didn't say anything to me."

"That's because there was nothing to say. Louise has a bad feeling about Randolph, which is neither here nor there as far as investigations are concerned, but she did witness Miranda giving Stanley a ration of grief during one of the scenes they shared."

"Okay, okay. You can look into that later. I found out something really important. Len Beckers used to date Miranda Lee. It was a few years back, but maybe there was still bad blood."

"How did you find that out? And what makes you think they still had issues?"

"At the beauty parlor. The hairdresser who has the chair next to my stylist is the sister of Len Beckers's deceased first wife. When she found out about Miranda's murder, she said it was awful and all of that, but . . . and here's the interesting part . . ."

"What? Get to it already."

"I am. Hold your horses. The stylist said she was really relieved her brother-in-law stopped dating Miranda."

"So what does that prove?"

"You're not letting me finish, Phee. She was relieved they stopped dating because she was afraid he was going to wind up killing her."

"Oh my gosh. Shouldn't she tell that to the sheriff's investigators?"

"Tell what? What's there to tell? She said Miranda was the kind of woman who could push someone over the edge. In this case, it would have been Len Beckers. *Would have.* We don't know for sure. That's where you come in."

"Me? You want me to meet with a potential killer?"

"In public. In a public place. Now, according to the list I gave you, the man belongs to the archery club. They practice every Saturday from two to five at the archery range off of Beardsley Boulevard. You can go today."

"An archery range? With bows and arrows? Wrong. Wrong. Wrong. Where else can I find him?"

"Uh. Let me see. I've got some notes in my pocket-book that I didn't put on the list. Give me a minute."

While my mother rummaged through her bag, I stood back and watched the endless flow of cars in and out of the parking lot of Bagels 'N More. By next month, the Canadians were sure to arrive for their usual five-month stint in Arizona, and finding a parking spot would be next to impossible. I was wondering just how early my mother and her friends were willing to wake up, when she finally finished routing through her bag.

"Here it is. I knew I wrote this down. Len Beckers is involved in all sorts of activities. He bowls with a league on Sundays at three-thirty at the RH Johnson Rec Center. Good timing. It doesn't interfere with rehearsals. Since you're not busy on Sundays, you can—"

"How do you know I'm not busy on Sundays? Sundays might be my busiest days."

"Well, are you?"

I groaned and shook my head.

"Good. Then it's settled. You can drive over to the bowling alley tomorrow, and when he's in between rolling a ball, you can talk to him."

"That's not going to be so easy. I mean, in front of everyone."

"It's that or the archery range."

"Fine. Fine. I'll think of something."

"Pretend you want to sign up to join his bowling league. That might work."

"The last time I bowled was before I gave birth to Kalese and, no, that wouldn't work. Look, don't worry about it. I'll come up with something."

"Just be careful. You don't want him dropping a heavy ball on your foot."

"No, he'll be too busy trying to stuff it in my mouth."

Just then a car pulled up behind my mother, and the driver waited to see if the spot was going to open up.

"I think we'd better get going, Mom. I'll let you know how things work out."

I wasn't sure how I was going to broach the subject of Miranda's suspicious death with Len Beckers, but I figured I had at least twenty-four hours to come up with something. Former boyfriends usually fell into two categories—they either wanted to talk about their exes or they didn't. I hoped Len fell into the first category.

The rest of the day was pretty mundane. I ran errands, picked up groceries and threw in a load of laundry. My mother would have been ecstatic to learn I did the wash when the low weekend rates were in effect.

At six-thirty, I finally sat on the couch, tore into a bag of popcorn and propped my feet on the coffee table. Turner Classic Movies was about to show one of my favorite movies, *The Ghost and Mrs. Muir*, when the phone rang. I made no effort to budge. Whoever it was could leave a message, and I'd get back to them. Unfortunately, the "whoever" was my mother, and her message was more like a bellow.

"Pick up your phone, Phee. I know you're home by now. We got a death threat. I'm holding. I'm holding. Get to your phone."

I shoved the coffee table back, tossed my bag of popcorn against one of the couch pillows, and raced to catch her call. "I'm here. I'm here. What's going on? Are you still at the theater?"

"Yes. We're all here. For the time being."

"Okay. What's going on? What death threat?"

"Remember those notes Myrna and I got? And the one Paula accused me of sending to Miranda?"

"Uh-huh. With the message 'And then there were none.'"

"Well, someone wrote that same message with bright red lipstick across the large mirror in the ladies' dressing room. Shirley saw it first when she unlocked the door."

"Oh no. Not Shirley. That must've sent her over the edge."

"She's way past that. Screaming hysterically. The sheriff's deputy on duty had all he could do to calm her down."

"Did this happen right away when you first got to the rehearsal?"

"No. The cast ran lines first, and then the crew arrived about an hour and a half later. That's when Shirley unlocked the dressing room doors because people were getting into costume. The director wanted to see how the costumes looked with the lighting. He was concerned that some of the clothing might be too drab."

"Uh-huh. Then what?"

"Like I said, Shirley unlocked both dressing room doors so the cast could get into costume. When she turned on the lights in the ladies' dressing room, that's when she saw the message. Up until that point, the door had been locked. She's the only one with a key. Except for the director and stage manager. They have master keys."

"I hate to say it, but maybe one of those guys wrote the message. What do you know about the stage manager? Maybe he was dating Miranda, too."

"Not likely. If he was dating anyone, it would be one of the male cast members."

"Oh. I see. . . . Well, that still doesn't mean he didn't have a motive. Same goes for the director."

"I doubt it was the director. He nearly blew his top when he read the message. Mostly he was upset because the entire incident took time away from practice."

"I suppose a crime lab could figure out what kind of lipstick it was."

"They don't have to. It's stage lipstick from Ben Nye. Marilyn Red LS-33 color, to be exact. The stage manager unlocked the cabinet where they keep the stage makeup. Shirley couldn't get past the heebie-jeebies that it was Miranda's ghost who left that message, and she refused to go near the cabinet. Honestly. It's a good thing your Aunt Ina isn't here, or she'd demand we hold a séance to confront the spirit. Anyway, Richard Garson, he's the stage manager, in case I forgot to tell you, pulled out the tray of lipsticks and guess what? The Marilyn Red was missing. Someone had to have taken it to scrawl that message across the mirror."

"You know that only leaves two possible suspects. Unless someone got into the theater the night before when there was no rehearsal and did it then. Is that possible?"

"The deputy said the same thing. Seems lots of people still have master keys to the theater that they never returned after their club events or performances were done. And the locks haven't been changed in over twenty years. Twenty years. Who's going to go that far back to see who might have a key?"

"What's happening now? You said you were calling from the theater."

"I am. The deputy took a few pictures of the mirror with his cell phone and phoned the incident in to his office. He asked everyone to keep their eyes open in case they spot the lipstick. Who's he kidding? Even the worst dunderhead isn't going to leave evidence lying around."

"Are they going to continue with the rehearsal?"

"Of course. But I doubt it will be a good one. Everyone's upset, and, other than Shirley, and possibly Cecilia, who are both positive it's Miranda's ghost, most of the cast and crew believe it's her killer who's doing this. My God, Phee. The very thought that a crazed serial killer is among us in this theater is enough to get my nerves rattling."

"Un-rattle them. It's not a psychopathic serial killer."

"How do you know? What makes you the expert?"

"Because a lunatic killer usually kills more than one person."

The minute I said that, I was sorry I did. My mother gasped, and I quickly tried to undo the damage.

"Um. Uh. Listen. Deranged killers don't take their victims in front of an audience. They look for a quiet, secluded place. I'm sure you'll be fine. Give me a call when you get home, okay?"

"Ah-hah! Now who's worried?"

I was about to add something when my mother quickly ended the call with, "That's Cliff. He's calling for act one, scene one, places. I'm in this scene with Sue Ellen. Talk to you later."

Chapter 12

My mother called at a little past eight. Other than being exhausted, she and her friends left the rehearsal unscathed. It seemed so odd to me that I was the one worrying about her instead of the other way around. Once she got past the disturbing incident, my mother wasted no time reminding me that Len Beckers was going to be at the bowling alley the next day.

"I know. I know. I already told you I'd go there. By the way, did any of those deputies on duty indicate how their investigation was coming along?"

"No. Only that they were following procedure and protocol and all that other nonsense. That tells me they haven't figured out a darn thing. In fact, we don't even know what really killed Miranda. Her death was ruled a homicide, but that's all we know. Even the papers dodged the issue. You don't suppose you could get Marshall or Nate to find out, do you?"

"Not unless they're officially hired on behalf of the family or someone. They can't just call the local authorities and demand to hear the details of an ongoing investigation."

"Yes, they can. Oh yes they can. They do that all the time on *Elementary*."

"That's because those people work for the police. Oh my God! What am I saying? It's a TV show, for heaven's sake."

"Okay. You said someone would have to hire a private eye. Find out how much it costs. I'll see if the book club ladies want to chip in."

"You're not serious, Mom, are you?"

"Well, the way those deputies are working on the case, we'll be lucky if any of us are left alive by opening night. It's not that I don't think you're doing a good job tracking down information, but let's face it, those bureaucratic offices are used to one thing and one thing only, and that's working with other bureaucratic offices."

"I wouldn't exactly call Williams Investigations a bureaucratic office."

"You wouldn't, but what do those deputies know? When you get to work on Monday, ask your boss about his going rate. And find out what he's learned so far. Oh, and tell me how it goes with Len Beckers."

"I'll have a typed report in triplicate on your desk by midweek, how's that?"

"Very funny, Phee."

"Um . . . are you rehearsing tomorrow?" I didn't want to sound nervous, but I was. Whoever was orchestrating those behind-the-scenes pranks at the theater could very well have something to do with killing Miranda.

"No. Sunday is still sacred for now. I don't think the director wants to mess with the church goers, pickleball players, and bowlers. Next rehearsal is Monday afternoon. The schedule's been completely changed.

We never know from one day to the next when we're rehearsing. Cliff sometimes calls for just scene rehearsals and not the entire act."

"But the buddy system is still in place, right?"

"Absolutely. And Myrna ordered two more 'Screamers.' One for me and one for Shirley. Say, do you want her to get you one, too?"

"No. I'll use my vocal chords if I have to scream. Try to get a good night's sleep, Mom. I'll talk to you this week."

I didn't know about my mother, but when my head hit the pillow, I was zonked out until the next morning. I got up for an early swim followed by a relaxing breakfast with some of the ladies I met in my development. Quite the contrast from yesterday. No one spoke with a mouthful of food, no one reached across the table to get the salt, and only one person spoke at a time.

It was strange balancing two different Arizona worlds—my mother's retirement community and the multigenerational neighborhood I was starting to call my own. I hopscotched into my mother's domain at a little past three with a sketchy idea of how I could get Len Beckers to divulge information about Miranda.

The guy was easy to recognize as I walked into the RH Johnson Lanes. He was the only one with a moustache and a decent physique. A number of leagues were apparently playing that afternoon. I figured as much by the color of the shirts they were wearing. Len's team was decked out in red and khaki.

Leaning against a small counter where candy bars and soft drinks were available for purchase, I eyeballed the men as they took turns warming up. The plan I'd devised for initiating a conversation with the guy was about as subtle as dropping an anvil on him. I was going to wait for an opportune moment and then get right to the point. No sense pretending to be interested in bowling when I could pretend to be an investigator.

Pin by pin, ball by ball, I watched the endless lineup of men take their turn at the lane. Len seemed pretty good by comparison. A few spares and one strike. The process was slow moving and monotonous. Maybe that was why I never liked bowling.

Just as my eyes were starting to blur, I heard an announcement: "Desert Scorpions and Bowling Boomers up in five minutes."

At that moment, the men stopped what they were doing and moved over to the small table by the lanes. A few of the bowlers headed in my direction and Len Beckers was one of them. He leaned over the counter and asked for a Milky Way. No sooner did he start to unwrap it when I took a step toward him.

"Excuse me, are you Len Beckers? I'm Phee Kimball with Williams Investigations, and I wondered if I could have a moment of your time." I was smooth, I was calm, and I was professional. I was also nervous as hell.

"One minute is about all I've got. My team is up next. What's this about?"

"Miranda Lee."

The guy stood perfectly still and looked right at me. "Go on."

"I understand you were cast along with her in the Footlighters' play. We're asking cast and crew members if they have any idea who might have wanted to kill her."

"I already gave my statement to Deputy Bowman."

Not about to get the brush off, I raised my voice

slightly. "And did you tell Deputy Bowman you used to date Miranda?"

"Hey, see here. That's none of your business, or theirs, for that matter."

"It is when it comes to motive and murder."

I was beginning to feel like the real deal, complete with glib responses. Too bad the palms of my hands were soaked in sweat. I clasped them together and refused to take my gaze off the guy. It was working.

He seemed rattled and started to edge away from the counter. "Let's step away from the counter, okay? I don't need the whole world to listen."

We moved farther from the snacks until we were almost by the door.

"So, what can you tell me, Mr. Beckers?"

"That I didn't kill her, for starters. Look, Miranda and I dated for a few months, but that was years ago. It was over between us. What possible reason would I have for murdering her?"

"Maybe there was still some friction between the two of you. Unresolved issues. That sort of thing." I was reaching for something. Anything at this point.

"No unresolved issues. No lingering or malingering issues. It was done when I walked away from her and ended the relationship. I'll put it plain and simple. Miranda was a pain in the ass. A royal pain, if you know what I mean. Nothing ever pleased that woman. Sure, she was a looker, but that faded fast once she got on my nerves."

"Did she get under your nerves recently?"

"Like I said, I didn't kill her, if that's what you're implying. And as far as getting under anyone's nerves, try talking to Stanley Krumpmeyer. If she managed to irritate anyone, it was him. Those two held up rehearsals all the time whenever they were on stage together. It became a big joke. Who was going to upstage who? Well, she won. Upstaged us all with her arm dangling over the catwalk and her head poetically tilted back like the final scene in a Greek tragedy. Is there anything else you want from me? I've no intentions of holding up the league bowling."

"No. That's fine. I appreciate your time, Mr. Beckers. If we require further information, we'll be in touch."

He started toward the lane and then stopped and turned back. "Miss Kimball, was it? I forgot to ask you. How did you know I'd be here today? On a Sunday. Bowling."

I paused in order to give myself a moment to think. "We wouldn't be a very good investigative firm if we couldn't locate the people we may need to speak with."

"All right then."

With that, he was on his way, and I darted out the door so he wouldn't see how nervous I really was. I couldn't wait to get home and throw on an old T-shirt and shorts. The last thing I felt like doing was spending another minute in Sun City West. As I drove north on RH Johnson Boulevard, I passed the Stardust Theater on my right. Mom said there was no rehearsal, yet a handful of cars were parked right by the theater entrance.

If this was a horror movie, someone would be screaming, "Don't go in there! Turn back!" Like the horror movie heroines, I didn't listen to my inner voice either. For some inexplicable reason, I decided to see what was going on in the theater and perhaps catch red-handed, whoever was "haunting" the place.

The foyer was dimly lit but had enough light for me to locate and open the door to the auditorium. The

houselights were on but only at the lowest setting.
Directly in front of me, on stage, a man was pacing
back and forth. Only the houselights illuminated the
stage. As far as I could tell, no one else was around. I
sunk into the nearest seat and waited to see what the
man was going to do. My foot was tapping automati-
cally, and my hands were starting to shake.

Suddenly, a voice reverberated throughout the
empty room. Something about coming to protect the
guests from a murderer. It was the classic, "Oh my
God, I feel a chill running up and down my spine,"
when I realized it was one of the actors who must have
snuck in here to practice his lines. Then what about
those other cars in the parking lot?

I listened intently for a minute or two while the guy
went on and on about a note left on the body and
"Three Blind Mice." Clearly, he was rehearsing, but
did those lines have anything to do with the other
notes and the message on the mirror? Maybe this guy
was taking his role a little too serious. Turning an
Agatha Christie play into a real murder. I sat there
paralyzed. A bizarre combination of fear and morbid
curiosity.

"You go now, Mr. Actor." It was a lady's voice in
broken English. "Anushka and me go too. Bathroom
all clean. We lock doors."

The man responded. "Mr. Tilden. Not Mr. Actor.
What about Daniel? Is he going to be around for a
while?"

"Daniel go. Drain not run water."

"Okay. I'll be out of here. Thanks for letting me
sneak in to practice. And let's keep this our own secret,
all right?"

"Secret. Yes. Is good play, no?"

I started to relax. It appeared as if Randolph Tilden Jr. had talked the cleaning staff into letting him inside the theater for a secret one-man rehearsal. Of course, it would be the perfect opportunity for someone to write cryptic messages on mirrors or remove certain costumes from their hangers. I desperately wanted to approach him but couldn't very well jump out of my seat and start asking questions. After all, I had no right to be in that building either. But if my timing was right, I could bump into him in the parking lot.

As Randolph exited stage left, I bolted out of my seat and made a beeline for the door to the foyer. Then I exited the same way I got in, careful not to disturb the small shim that had held the door open in the first place. I didn't think anything unusual about it when I first arrived since people propped doors open all the time.

By the time Randolph walked out the door, I was already back in my car watching him make his way to his. Behind him, two middle-aged cleaning women were carefully locking the theater door. I waited until the guy was a good twenty feet from his vehicle when I jumped out of mine and waved to him.

"Excuse me. Did I miss the rehearsal?"

"What?"

His expression reminded me of one of those Norman Rockwell paintings where the kid gets caught with his hand in the cookie jar.

I asked him again. "Did I get here too late for the rehearsal?"

"Um, no. I mean, no. There was no rehearsal. I got the information wrong myself. I was just leaving."

"Phooey. I was hoping I could speak with someone

regarding the unfortunate incident that took place in the theater."

"Are you referring to Miranda Lee's murder?"

By now Randolph had walked a few feet toward me so there was no need to shout on either of our parts.

"Yes. I'm with Williams Investigations. Sophie Kimball. And you are?"

"Randolph Tilden Jr. I happen to be in the play."

"Then perhaps you won't mind telling me if you noticed anything unusual between Miss Lee and the other cast members?"

"Unusual? The woman was . . . how shall I put this . . . she was a first-class B-I-T—"

"You don't have to go any further, Mr. Tilden. I can spell. Do you mind elaborating on your perception of Miss Lee?"

"My perception? It was everyone's perception. I suggest you speak with the director, Cliff Edwards. He'll explain how difficult the woman was to work with. And then there's Stanley Krumpmeyer. Miranda and Stanley were always having words. Of course, compared to the rows that Miranda and Cliff had, her interactions with Stanley were quite cordial."

"I see. Anyone else she had problems with?"

"The first director. Ellowina Bice. Lovely lady. Tall, elegant presence, forceful and knowledgeable. Knows how to shoot a gun, too. She practices at the Ben Avery Shooting Range on Black Canyon Road every Sunday. I took my nephews there once and ran into her. Anyway, she knew the theater inside and out. Shame she got food poisoning and had to relinquish the position to Mr. Edwards."

I hadn't thought about Ellowina Bice since my

mom told me about the food poisoning/possible salmonella.

"Yes. I heard about that. Does anyone know how she's doing?"

"I heard she was discharged from the hospital. I would imagine she's at home recuperating, or maybe recuperating with her family. Those food-borne illnesses can take months to leave one's system."

"Uh-huh. I've heard that, too. Before you head out, Mr. Tilden, can you think of anyone who might have had a motive to kill Miranda Lee?"

Randolph took a slow deep breath as if preparing to deliver the soliloquy from *Hamlet*. "In the theater, one comes across all sorts of players. Self-serving, self-aggrandizing, self-centered. Miranda was all of those and more. Still, that's hardly a motive for murder. Murder rips into the soul. It had to be rage or revenge. Something was smoldering below the surface. Blackmail perhaps? Extortion? Whatever it was, it erupted on that catwalk and most likely had nothing at all to do with the play."

I felt as if I had been privy to a theatrical performance without the need to purchase a ticket.

It took me a good ten seconds or more to respond. "That was quite an in-depth explanation. I appreciate your time, Mr. Tilden. Good luck with the play."

"You mean 'break a leg.' It's considered bad luck to wish actors good luck."

"Oh. Well then, break a leg." *Or whatever body part you choose.* "Again, thank you for your time."

He nodded and walked directly to his car. My mother and her friends weren't all that freaked out when I'd wished them good luck with the play. Then again, none of them were retired theater professors from back east. I honestly didn't think Randolph had any reason to murder Miranda, but the more I heard about Cliff and Stanley, the more I began to wonder about their motives. Especially when it came to rage.

In spite of an early morning swim, I still needed to cool off with a shower when I got back from the bowling alley and theater. It was no longer as humid as it had been during the summer, but dry heat was equally miserable. It just evaporated faster on your skin, leaving behind an unwelcóme odor.

No sooner had I toweled off and thrown on a pair of old sweat shorts and a shirt when the phone rang. It didn't take a clairvoyant to figure out who it was.

"Don't hold back. Tell me. What did you find out? Was Len Beckers harboring a grudge or something against Miranda? Was it enough for him to kill her?"

"Hello, Mom. I thought I said I'd give you a call this week. I'm still dripping wet from getting out of the shower."

Apparently, exaggerations didn't work that well with Harriet Plunkett.

"No one is dripping wet in Arizona. Even indoor air will dry you in minutes. What did you find out?"

I proceeded to tell my mother about the two encounters—the one she had orchestrated and the serendipitous one with Randolph Tilden Jr. at the Stardust Theater. Somehow, she didn't seem surprised by their reactions.

"Listen closely, Phee. Both of them pointed a finger at Stanley Krumpmeyer. And Randolph used the word 'rage' when he referred to the murder. If people can go crazy behind the wheels of their cars and pull out guns at drivers who cut them off or don't signal, then think what someone might do if they had to deal with Miranda's actions. Maybe it was theater rage."

"Theater rage? There's no such thing. Besides, Randolph was being overly theatrical. And how would Stanley have known Miranda would be on the catwalk? I'm thinking more along the lines of a premeditated murder."

"Like something Len Beckers would do since he had a relationship with her?"

"Uh-huh. I got the sense he dropped her like a hot potato but wasn't so distraught that he stomped on it until it was mashed."

I couldn't believe I had used a food analogy. I must have been getting hungry.

"Baked potato, mashed potato, the thing is, you should talk to Stanley and find out what he has to say. Find out if he has a temper. And do it in public."

"I'm working all week, or have you forgotten? It's not like last time, when I was here on vacation."

"You'll find the time, Phee. You did when Aunt Ina's master chef was murdered."

True. I had helped to expose Chef Roland LeDoux's killer, but it was more a matter of dumb luck than practiced skill. Not to mention the genuine fear that my aunt would have a nervous breakdown if I didn't. "Fine," I said. "I'll see what your list says about Stanley's schedule."

"Good. And don't forget to ask your boss about what we discussed earlier."

"Hiring them?"

"Ask about a senior discount."

The call lasted another few minutes, and I had to admit, my mother was right. When I put the receiver down, my hair was absolutely dry.

Chapter 13

"Your mother really wants to hire us to look into that murder?"

Nate was leaning against the door frame of my office, coffee cup in hand, grinning. A typical Monday morning.

"I'm afraid so. Those women are absolutely petrified but are too stubborn to quit the play. It's the work ethic from their generation."

"Hey, that's my generation, too."

"Oops, I—"

Before Nate could answer, Marshall leaned his head into the office as well. "What am I missing?"

"My mother is convinced the sheriff's department isn't getting anywhere with Miranda's murder and realizes I can do just so much. So, she thought if she and her book club ladies all chipped in, they could hire this firm to find out the actual cause of death and any pertinent information. Before either of you say anything, I want to make something perfectly clear. This wasn't my idea. And if you do decide to get involved, don't say I didn't warn you first. Working for my mother and her friends is akin to stepping into quicksand. You'll be gobbled up in no time."

Nate didn't say a word and neither did Marshall. The two of them looked at each other for what seemed like eons. I wasn't sure if they were going to laugh or run the other way. Finally, they both nodded. Not enthusiastically, but definite nods. Nate walked over to my desk and sat in one of the chairs while Marshall muttered something about needing a cup of coffee and quickly left the room.

"I don't have a problem with this, kiddo. And neither does Marshall. But I don't want to take money from your mother or her friends. Call it pro bono. We can look into it, but your mom will have to sign an official contract. That gives us the legal right to proceed and contact the sheriff's office."

"You, of all people, know what she's like, Nate. I wasn't kidding. This could turn out to be a nightmare for you. And it'll take you away from your other clients."

"Nah. I think all she's looking for is some information, and we can get that without too much trouble. Give her a call and let her know Augusta will be emailing over a contract."

"She'll insist on paying."

"Fine. I'll give her a discount."

"By the way, I found out some information that might help you get a profile on Miranda Lee. Actually, it's more like the local scuttlebutt, but here goes. According to my mother, Miranda was married twice. Her first husband died under suspicious circumstances. One of those 'off the cruise ship balconies' or something like that. It happened years ago, before Miranda moved to Sun City West."

"Hmm. That's rather interesting. If indeed it's the truth and not a fabrication."

"Oh my gosh, Nate. If it *is* true, then what if one of the cast or crew members turn out to be a relative of her first husband and finally got the revenge they wanted for his death?"

"I'd say that was a terrific movie plot, although not altogether out of the question. You said she was married twice. Who was the other lucky fellow?"

"I don't know. I mean, my mother doesn't know and neither do the other ladies. Miranda was using a different last name, but now uses her middle name, Lee, as her last name. What a lot of paperwork. I decided to keep my married name for my daughter's sake when my husband and I divorced centuries ago. I doubt I'll be changing it anytime soon."

I turned to reach for my cup of coffee and didn't see Marshall return to the room. I did, however, hear his voice, and I froze.

"Who's not changing names?" he asked. "I keep missing everything."

"The only thing you missed was the fact you and your boss are taking on a new and challenging cadre of clients."

"Great."

"And there's one more thing. At least one of them will want you to do some ghostbusting as well."

"Like Dan Aykroyd and Bill Murray?"

I took a quick gulp of coffee. "You won't be that lucky. More like Shirley Johnson and Cecilia Flanagan. They're convinced Miranda's spirit won't leave the theater."

Nate stood and gave Marshall a pat on the shoulder.

"This one's for you, buddy. Find out all the details. And you thought Mankato was interesting."

"Miranda's spirit?" Marshall asked. "Really? They think she's haunting the place?"

I nodded. "Yep, that's their latest observation. Or should I say 'speculation'?"

"I'd better pull up a chair."

Marshall stayed in my office long enough for me to bring him up to date on the book club ladies and on the progress of my makeshift investigation. He was pretty certain he'd be able to find out the cause of death and the status of the official investigation. That crisp apple smell lingered in the air when he left the room, and I literally had to force myself to stop day-dreaming and focus on my accounting.

I figured Monday afternoon's rehearsal must have gone well because I didn't receive any frantic calls from my mother. It wasn't until I pulled up a late-day email from her that I learned the rehearsal had been moved to the next day. Something about Cliff and a dentist appointment. My mother also mentioned that Williams Investigations had sent her an official contract and that "it was a good one."

I'll say one thing for my boss. He can be quite clever. According to the contract, Williams Investigations offered an introductory special for new clients, plus a family and friends discount, as well as a senior citizen discount, bringing the grand total for the month to thirty-nine ninety-nine. Split six ways, it would amount to less than seven dollars each. I had all I could do to stop laughing. The hourly rate for our services was more than the total. But if Nate had offered to track down the information for free, my mother would've been convinced he wouldn't give it his full attention.

"So, are we competing with T-Mobile, now?" I asked Nate as he headed home for the day.

"Ah, so your mother must have liked the family and friends discount."

"If she knew what the rates really were, she'd have a coronary. Well, at least you or Marshall can now find out more about the cause of death."

"Sooner than you think. Marshall headed out to Peoria on a missing person's case, but he plans to stop by the sheriff's office before he calls it quits for the day. Speaking of which, shouldn't you be on your way out, too? Augusta's already gone home."

"I have a few odds and ends to finish up, and then I'll lock up and enjoy a quiet evening in Vistancia."

And miraculously, that was exactly what I did. I enjoyed a peaceful evening at home with a late day swim and a frozen pizza.

I found out early the next day that the only thing clean about Miranda's cause of death was the toxicology report. Apparently the woman suffered a bump to the back of the head. The blow could have been the cause, but the medical examiner thought it had occurred after she was already dead. Perhaps from falling backward. Then there were the ligature marks on her neck. Unlike marks from a rope, cord, or wire, the ones on her neck came from her own necklace, as if it had gotten tangled in the maze of electrical cords and inadvertently strangled her. But how did she get tangled in the first place? And if that wasn't enough to throw a monkey wrench into the cause of death, possible electrocution was.

While one of Miranda's hands was clearly dangling over the catwalk, the other was holding the male end of a cord that appeared to be frayed. Had she tried to plug it in so that she could see for herself if the spotlight would surround her on stage? Was that what killed her? And shouldn't there have been burn marks?

When the deputy on duty at the Stardust Theater told my mother the investigation was ongoing, I guessed what he really meant was that he wasn't about to divulge anything to her. His department, however, shared what they knew with Marshall, even though it wasn't much.

"I'm sorry, Phee. This is all we've got for now."

Marshall had this adorable schoolboy sheepishness going for him when he spoke to me that morning. I was so taken by the sincerity on his face, that I didn't say a word and waited for him to continue.

"Don't worry. We'll figure it out. I can make myself useful now, too. Starting with a quick chitchat at this afternoon's rehearsal. I was able to get ahold of the stage manager, Richard Garson. According to him, they're rehearsing from three to seven. Care to stop by when you get off?"

"Um. I don't think that's such a great idea. Len and Randolph think I'm really an investigator, and I know my mother's friends are going to squelch that ruse the minute I step into the theater. I need to do my snooping on the periphery."

"Speaking of which, I've uncovered an interesting tidbit for you, thanks to the Maricopa County Sheriff's Department. Miranda Lee was born Miranda Lee Shumway. She dropped the Shumway when she married her first husband, the unfortunate Leonard Milestone. Poor guy never even survived the honeymoon. Died while trekking the Andes."

"The Andes? Like in Peru? I heard he fell off the balcony on a cruise ship."

"Nope. Slipped somewhere on the Inca Trail."

"You don't suppose—"

"No. It was a long time ago, and, according to the report filed with the Peruvian authorities, it was an accident."

"What about her second husband? Did you find out anything about him?"

Marshall was literally grinning from ear to ear. "Oh yeah. Hold on to your seat for this one. Her second husband is none other than the esteemed director from Peoria, Cliff Edwards."

"Really? Cliff Edwards?" I could barely contain myself. "Oh my gosh! That would explain all the bickering going on between them. According to Myrna, it even got physical with Miranda slapping the guy."

"Seems like this Miranda created a maelstrom wherever she went."

"Given her past relationship with Cliff, he might have had a darn good reason to kill her. I'd put him on the suspect list for sure. As the director, he had access to every area in the building. No one would think it unusual for him to be up in the catwalk. Maybe he even lured her up there."

"From what I've heard, if anyone was going to be doing the luring, it would've been her. Anyway, no one's off the hook for now. Well, I've got to work on a few other cases. Talk to you later. And if you change your mind about this afternoon, you'll know where to find me."

Was he dropping a not-so-subtle hint? Did he want me to join him, or was it one of those open-ended things? Darn it. I was too old to play these junior high games. Next thing you knew I'd be writing "Mrs. Sophie Gregory" on notebook paper.

I was looking forward to another noneventful night back home when the next *Mousetrap* bombshell hit. Marshall called me at a little past four from the Stardust Theater.

"Don't get upset, Phee. I wanted to call before your mother or any of her friends got to the phone. There's been a minor accident at the theater. And I'm stressing the word 'minor.'"

In the background I heard Shirley's unmistakable voice shrieking. Something about Miranda's spiteful spirit.

"What's happened? Is everyone all right?"

"Yeah. Everyone's fine. The rehearsal got off to a late start because the director needed the lighting adjusted and had to meet with that crew. I was able to speak with one of the actors, Chuck Mitchenson, for a few minutes. Not a wealth of information there. Anyway, the rehearsal got under way with act one, scene one. Sue Ellen came on stage first, followed by Gordon Web. Gordon had to cross in front of a small table when, all of a sudden, he fell through a trapdoor that had been left open."

"Didn't he see it? Didn't anyone see it?"

"No. There was a small braided rug covering it up. Poor guy fell right through, taking most of the rug with him. He's okay, though."

Shirley's voice was getting louder in the background, and hers wasn't the only one. I hoped Marshall was able to hear me.

"Sounds like bedlam behind you."

"It is. Like I said, everyone's fine. But that doesn't mean they're not shaken up. I suppose actors use these trapdoors all the time because Gordon landed on some foam cushioning and not the hard floor. Do you know if this play calls for one of the actors to use a trapdoor?"

"I don't think so. You'd better check with someone who's familiar with the script. How's Gordon taking it?"

"Believe it or not, he's not nearly as razzled as the others. This Sue Ellen Blair lady is crying her eyes out. She's convinced the killer is after her for taking over Miranda's role."

"Oh brother. I can see this is going to be a long night for my mother."

"Right now, the deputy on duty is questioning the crew members, specifically the set crew and the prop crew about the incident."

"Well at least no one got hurt. What's your take on all of this?"

"Hard to say. Either someone is dead serious about sabotaging this play, or whoever killed Miranda Lee is trying to make it look like it wasn't meant to be a single murder."

"So you don't buy the serial killer thing either."

"Nope. Whoever's responsible is taking the focus off of Miranda and spreading it all over the place."

"Why? That doesn't make sense."

"It does if they're trying to conceal the motive for her death. By putting everyone else in jeopardy, or making it seem that way, the killer has effectively distanced the original murder because everyone will be scared stiff they're next."

"Do me a favor, will you, Marshall? Tell my mother I'm stopping by the theater on my way home."

"I figured as much. See you in a while."

I gave Nate a quick lowdown on what had happened the minute I got off the phone. He shared the same perspective as Marshall and the same concerns. "Be careful. And stay in sight. You *do* carry a small flashlight, don't you?"

"This is scary. You're sounding just like my mother."

Chapter 14

I kept telling myself that as long as the book club ladies refrained from telling everyone I was an accounting clerk and not an investigator, then Len and Randolph wouldn't bat an eye when I showed up at the theater. After all, it would seem pretty logical that I'd be conversing with another investigator in my office. And so what if I was an accounting clerk? I still worked for Williams Investigations, and, for all they knew, snooping around could have been part of my job description.

No one really noticed me that first day when Miranda's body was discovered and I'd snuck in. I suppose the cast and crew had still been in shock. This time was different. A few of them, including my mother's friends, were in panic mode, while Herb's pinochle buddies from the lighting and construction crew seemed downright annoyed.

It was a quarter past six when I entered the building. When I walked into the auditorium, the stage was empty. A few people were clustered together near the stage, and I imagined the rest were backstage or in the greenroom, the technical term for the small waiting room/lounge that the actors used.

Above me, I heard men's voices. Obviously, they weren't too concerned about who might be listening.

I immediately recognized Bill's voice. It was uncensored and loud. "I'm telling you, there's a damn lunatic around here, and he or she is going to get all of us killed if we don't do something about it. I'm thinking maybe we should booby-trap the catwalk so if they decide to climb up here, they won't get too far."

"Cripes, Bill. We'll wind up killing someone. What were you thinking, anyway?" It was Herb's voice. At least he didn't look down and see me. I wasn't in the mood to hear "Hi, cutie pie."

Bill continued to spout off his plan. "Like the play says, 'mousetraps,' only in this case a few rat traps here and there."

"Forget it. Hey, Kevin, what did you do with that penlight?"

"I'll tell you what I'd like to do with it, but seeing as we're with mixed company down there, I'll keep quiet. I'm sick of these damn interruptions. I've got a life, too, you know. I told my wife I'd be home in time for dinner. Now we'll be lucky if we get out of here by eight."

I walked straight ahead, figuring I'd go backstage and locate my mother and Marshall. I mean, where else could they be? I took the steps to the right of the stage when, all of a sudden, the director and stage manager walked across the set followed by Marshall and the deputy on duty.

"Psst! Marshall! Psst!"

He spun his head around and saw me. "Phee, come on up. Might as well join us." Then, turning to the others he said, "Phee's with our office."

Yay! I have the Seal of Approval to be here.

A collective mumble followed as I took my place on the stage.

Cliff was pointing to the small rug and shaking his head. "I don't get it. If this was supposed to be an attempted murder, the perpetrator failed miserably. Even without the foam cushioning, the worst that might happen is a broken bone."

The deputy looked down at the rug as if it was concealing the Grand Canyon. "When was the last time you used the stage?"

Cliff spoke up immediately. "On Saturday. For rehearsal. And when we left, that trapdoor was secured. The actors had been walking back and forth across the stage all afternoon."

This time Marshall spoke. "What about the rug? Was it there on Saturday?"

Cliff glanced down and shrugged. "A rug was supposed to be there, but I don't know if it was. Guess I overlooked that detail. Let me get one of the prop crew."

While the men milled around waiting for someone from the prop crew to emerge, I motioned for Marshall to step back near the curtains so I could tell him something. Keeping my voice barely below a whisper forced him to be mere inches from me. I swear my heartbeat was louder than my whisper.

"There was no rehearsal yesterday. And on Sunday, Randolph Tilden Jr. had the stage to himself. Remember? He could have opened the door and put the rug back down. Who would have known? Not the cleaners."

At that moment, Louise Munson appeared on stage, and I don't know what was shaking more, her head or her body. Her voice practically cracked. "When that rug went down, the door was closed. Completely closed. We wouldn't place a rug over a hole in the stage."

The deputy rolled his head, more in exasperation than consolation. "Now, now, no one's saying you did. Calm down."

That was the last thing Louise was about to do. She started tapping her foot and looking all around. Cliff walked toward her and told her everything was okay and that the prop crew wasn't being blamed.

"Well I should certainly hope not!" Paula Darren blared. She strutted across the stage until she stood directly in front of Richard. "There are two more of these," she said, pointing to the trapdoor. "Have you checked them out? As the stage manager, you should be aware of every nuance."

Richard looked as if he was about to strangle Paula in front of all of us. His face turned beet red, and he clasped his hands together as if preventing them from doing the deed. "What do you take us for? Blithering idiots? That was the first thing we did. I mean, after we made sure Gordon wasn't hurt."

Marshall moved away from the curtains until he was inches from Cliff and Richard. "Can one of you tell me where the other trapdoors are located?"

Cliff nodded and turned his back to the audience. "One's on upstage right and the other on upstage left."

Marshall sighed. "Hey, for those of us who aren't all that familiar with the theater business, where exactly is 'upstage'?"

"It's toward the back curtains," Cliff said. "Downstage is by the audience. Look, from now on, we've got a new protocol for the stage manager. Those trapdoors are to be checked when the cast and crew enter the theater and again right before we begin rehearsing.

And that's not all. Crew chiefs are going to check their areas for any signs of tampering when they arrive."

No sooner did Cliff finish with his latest directive when Kevin's voice all but shook the walls.

"Hey, down there! Are we going to start any time soon? I want to eat my dinner while it's still warm and someone's going to serve it to me."

Under his breath Marshall said, "Oh brother. Marriage of the year."

I tried not to laugh as Cliff shouted back to Kevin.

"Hold your horses. We want to make sure there's not another accident."

A few seconds later, Stanley Krumpmeyer stuck his head out from the stage left wing and shouted, "The cast is getting really restless back there. What do you want me to tell them?"

"Tell them we're finishing up." Then, facing the deputy, Cliff added, "We are, aren't we?"

"Yeah. For now. I'll need to complete a report so don't plan on leaving once the rehearsal is done. Can't speak for the private investigators, though."

Marshall took another look at the trapdoor and then paced five or six steps past it until he was almost across the stage to the wing.

"If you don't mind, I'll speak with some of the crew backstage, and then we'll get out of your hair."

"Fine. Fine," Cliff replied. "There's a door on stage right behind the curtains. Follow the noise, and you'll find the cast and crew." Then, turning to Richard, he said, "Act one, scene one, five minutes to curtain. Notify everyone."

Marshall and I walked into the greenroom seconds before the stage manager made his announcement. Other than Randolph, who was seated in a corner by himself, the rest of the cast was gathered in the middle of the room on a brown couch and the well-worn chairs that surrounded it.

My mother jumped up the minute she saw me. "Phee! It's about time. That could have been your mother down that trapdoor."

"You *are* my mother, and you seem to be in one piece. Whoever opened that trapdoor intended it to be for one of the cast members who appear on stage before you."

"Tell that to Shirley."

"Oh, for heaven's sake. Don't tell me she's still going on about a ghost. Ghosts can't open trapdoors. Ghosts . . . What am I even saying? Ghosts don't exist."

"Shirley believes the malevolent spirit of the undead can inhabit someone's body."

"Terrific. She should swap stories with Joe Hill."

"Who's that? Is he on one of the crews?"

Marshall shook his head and smiled. "It's Stephen King's son, who also writes gothic horror, and your daughter's trying to be funny."

"Seriously, Mom, I don't think anyone is after you, in particular, but the director is going to be speaking with all the crew chiefs about checking things over and taking precautions."

My mother gave me a cursory nod and looked directly at Marshall. "Be honest, do I need to up my life insurance policy?"

"I agree with Phee. I think you'll be okay, but the sooner we can find out who killed Miranda Lee, the sooner this nonsense around here will stop."

"Two minutes to curtain!"

Richard opened the door and panned the greenroom. "Places!"

Sue Ellen stood up from her spot on the couch and headed to the door. If Marshall hadn't seen her and taken a step back, she would have crashed right into him.

"Sorry." Her voice was sweet and apologetic. She kept going, no time to turn around.

Gordon followed her, only he was faster and had an unobstructed path.

Marshall tapped me on the elbow and motioned for us to leave the room. "I think that's our cue to let the show go on."

"You're not leaving yet, are you?" My mother had now maneuvered herself to the doorway and stood there like one of those nightclub bouncers.

"Mom, Marshall can't very well talk to the cast and crew while a run-through is going on. At least during scene rehearsals he can pull people aside."

"The next scene rehearsal is tomorrow from two to four. Then a run-through at seven."

Marshall jotted down the information on his phone. It was either an app or a feature I hadn't figured out yet on mine.

"Mrs. Plunkett, I know some of the cast and crew members are anxious to get out of here as soon as the rehearsal is over, but do you know if the others go out somewhere to wind down? You know, have a drink and schmooze? People are more willing to talk when they're relaxed."

"With the exception of Kevin, who, if you haven't noticed, hasn't missed too many home-cooked meals, the other guys stop by Curley's Sports Grill. It's less than a mile from here, across from the hospital."

My mother was a regular road yenta, but this surpassed anything to date. "How do you know that, Mom?"

"How do you think? From Herb. He and his cronies complain that they can't meet women, yet, where do they go? To the one sports bar in town where women wouldn't be caught dead entering. Now if they went to the Homey Hut, like we do, they could enjoy a nice slice of pie and a cup of coffee."

"I don't think a slice of pie and a cup of coffee is what they're after."

My mother motioned for us to stop talking so she could hear the actors on the stage. "I'm on in a few minutes. Tell the truth, is that what you two are going to do? Hang out in a dingy bar and wait for those men to show up?"

Growing up under Harriet Plunkett's roof, I was used to this line of questioning.

Marshall, however, seemed taken completely off guard. "We, um, er, well, it's not like we'd, or I'd, be hanging out there for hours. I thought maybe Phee and I could grab a bite to eat and then go over there."

Phee and I. In the same sentence. A bite to eat. I think this is the closest I'll get to a date with him.

My mother took a deep breath. "I see. Find out everything you can from those bumbling buffoons. They've got a bird's-eye view up on that catwalk, not to mention what Wayne can hear from backstage when he's not putting glow tape on the floor, pounding a hammer, or fiddling with the sound effects."

"You didn't tell me Wayne was doing sound effects. You said construction. And what's glow tape?"

"In this place, if you know how to use a hammer and a screwdriver, they figure you can turn a knob up and down for noise. And glow tape is tape that glows in the dark. They put it on the floor for the actors to follow when the lights are out. It lasts four to eight hours before they have to do something to it. I wasn't paying that much attention when Ellowina explained it to us. My gosh, that seems like ages ago. Call me later, Phee. I think I'm on."

My mother left Marshall and me standing in the hallway a few feet from the back of the stage.

He inched closer to me and spoke softly so as not to disturb the rehearsal. "Uh, I should have asked you sooner. Do you want to get something to eat and then find a way to weasel into the conversation at Curley's, or would you rather head home and leave me to fend for myself with the bumbling buffoons?"

"I wouldn't wish that on anyone, especially you. Of course I'll join you. Besides, I'm starving. You don't think Curley's is going to sully my reputation, do you?"

"Sully your reputation? That's an interesting word for it. No, your reputation's safe. Besides, you've got everyone convinced you're a detective."

"Yeah. About that . . ."

"Shh. It might just work for us."

Chapter 15

There was a terrific mom and pop pizza place not far from Curley's, so we headed over there. Marshall insisted on paying for our meat lover's pizza and drinks, the hallmark of a real date, except, I knew it wasn't. The crowd consisted of young families, groups of teens, and a few older couples.

My gaze darted all over the place, summing up the action. "Guess we picked the local hot spot, huh?"

Marshall nodded, took a sip of his Coke, and reached for another slice. "Looks that way. And if I have to watch the waiter walk by with another pitcher of beer, I'll go nuts. Normally, I like to have a brew with pizza, but since we'll need to blend in at Curley's, I don't need a head start."

"I'm more of a Coca-Cola person, but I should be weaning myself away from all that sugar."

"For a healthier lifestyle maybe, but not because you need to."

I was completely taken back by his offhanded compliment and fumbled around for an answer. Nothing came out right. "Um, er, well, thanks . . . I suppose. So . . . do you have a plan for how we're going to approach the pinochle guys? Oh, and I should warn you, Herb fancies himself a real ladies' man, so don't be surprised if you hear him call me 'cutie pie' or 'honey bunch.' I've learned to ignore it."

"Hey, as long as he doesn't call *me* those names, we'll be all right."

We took our time eating the pizza and managed to consume the entire pie. Another slice and I would've needed to call a local garage for a crane to hoist me out of the booth.

"Wow. I must have really been hungry. Usually I don't eat that much." *Who am I kidding? He's lucky I didn't put a slice in each hand.*

"Don't worry about it. You don't see me making apologies for my appetite. It was a great pizza. We should stop by here again."

On a date?

Marshall leaned back and stretched. "Listen, the only approach I have to get those guys to open up is a non-approach."

"Huh?"

"I figured we could tell them we stopped by for a drink because the place was nearby and we wanted to unwind. We'll ask if we can join them, unless, of course, we arrive before they walk in and, in that case, we'll be the ones to invite them over. Either way, it'll work out."

He was right. It did work out. We got to Curley's before the men, so we commandeered one of the long tables directly across from the bar and ordered two beers, one of which was nonalcoholic, for me. It was easy to see who came through the door, and one thing became perfectly clear. I was the only woman in the place who wasn't wearing a low-cut tank top and tight leggings.

Four or five gray-haired men, who looked as if they belonged to a geriatric biker gang, walked inside the place. I tried not to be obvious as I watched them cram into a booth. "Interesting clientele, huh?"

"Oh yeah," Marshall mumbled, but I think he was looking elsewhere.

We didn't have to wait long. A few seconds after the biker crew sat down, Herb, Wayne, Bill, and Kenny made their appearance. I figured none of them had meals waiting for them at home like Kevin did. Bill was grumbling as soon as the door flew open. He was so loud the sound emanating from the eight or nine televisions on the walls couldn't drown him out. Soccer cheers, golf statistics, and pro football were no match for him.

"Must have been a rough rehearsal," Marshall called out as he waved them over.

Herb immediately waved back. "Well, what do you know? Didn't expect to see you here."

He took the chair opposite mine and plunked himself down, leaving a decent-size gap between his stomach and the table. The other guys grunted their hellos and made themselves comfortable, too.

Wayne shot his arm up in the air and got the attention of our server. "Bring us a round, will you, Zoey?"

A pencil-thin woman with spiked hair and long, dangling earrings shouted back, "You got it, Wayne!" From a distance, it was hard to tell if she was fifteen or fifty.

Kenny ran his fingers through his hair and moaned, "If I have to put up with one more night of Sue Ellen's crying, I swear she'll be the next one dangling on the catwalk."

If Kenny appeared to be ticked, Bill was worse.

"What the hell. That wasn't half as bad as that chowder head Chuck forgetting his lines every other second. Geez, we're only weeks away from opening night. When does he plan on learning them?"

Marshall gave me a quick look, and I knew he had his opening. "It's probably all that tension from the unresolved murder. These cases always seem to drag on and then, all of a sudden, something clicks and we've got our culprit."

"Yeah, well, it can't click fast enough," Bill said. "Sue Ellen was bawling her eyes out again, convinced the open trapdoor was meant for her. What I don't understand is why Ellowina Bice cast that Mitchenson guy in the first place. Hells bells, I could do a better job."

The guy was on a roll and he kept going. "And I'll tell you something else. I'm getting sick and tired of all that poppycock about Miranda's ghost. Next time someone thinks her spirit is in the building, I'm going to ask it to get to work like the rest of us. Yeah, sure, the building's got some mechanical issues like the heating and AC, but all older theaters do."

"What about the AC?" I asked. "Did it get fixed?"

Herb leaned his elbows on the table and answered before Bill got the chance. "If by fixed, you mean did Melvin and Sons spend the entire afternoon there yesterday, then the answer is yes. So far, so good. I talked to Daniel, the maintenance guy, when I got to rehearsal today, and he filled me in. He also mentioned finding some of his tools out of place, but, since nothing was missing, he let it go. He thought maybe one of us on the stage crew needed to borrow something."

Wayne started to speak when Zoey appeared with

tall, frosted glasses and a pitcher of beer. Up close, I still couldn't guess her age.

"Let me know when you're ready for another one."

"We're ready," Kenny said. "Might as well bring it."

As Zoey left, Wayne continued where he left off. "Geez, Herb. Didn't you bother to tell him we've got our own stuff? All sorts of tools. I'll say one thing for the Footlighters, they didn't skimp on that stuff. Power tools, too."

"Still doesn't mean someone didn't go rooting through Daniel's toolbox."

"Well, it wasn't one of us," Kenny replied.

His last remark was followed by a chorus of "yeahs" as the men poured themselves glasses of beer and started drinking.

Marshall took advantage of the brief lull. "Look, you guys are up on that catwalk or backstage all the time. Other than people forgetting their lines, or, sorry Phee, hysterical women, have you noticed any-thing else that would give us a clue about Miranda's murder?"

Kenny leaned across the table, eyeballed everyone and spoke. "Stanley Krumpmeyer threatened to kill her."

Marshall practically leapt from his seat. "What? Why didn't you tell this to the sheriff's deputy?"

"Because I wasn't the one who heard it. Kevin did. He told me about it a few days later. Miranda was still alive then."

"Did he just come right out and say he'd kill her?"

"No, according to Kevin, Stanley and Miranda were having one of their typical arguments and Stanley said, 'I'll be taking my bow over your cold, dead body.'

We thought it was kind of funny at the time. Now . . . not so much."

I gave Marshall's arm a slight shake and whispered, "My mother said Louise also witnessed something similar."

Marshall took another swallow of his beer and asked if anyone knew anything about Stanley Krumpmeyer.

Turned out they all knew the same thing, and Bill said it out loud, "You mean 'the voice of WSCW, one-oh-three-point-nine FM?'"

Marshall gave me a funny look, and I explained. "Sun City West's got its own radio station. It's run by the broadcast club and comes on the air mornings from seven to noon. They play all sorts of requests, but you have to bring your own CDs ahead of time. They also conduct interviews with people from different clubs or sports leagues. Cliff Edwards has been on a few times to promote the play, and, according to my mother, some of the actors will be doing a scene as a teaser right before ticket sales."

"I take it Stanley is the driving force behind this radio station?" Marshall asked.

"Don't know about that, but he's bound to be the loudest," Wayne said. "That's why watching him and Miranda go at it was such a hoot until she wound up dead."

Marshall took a quick swallow of beer and cleared his throat. "Tell me, was there anything at all out of the ordinary the night before her body was found? Anything odd during rehearsal?"

Bill tapped his teeth as if he was trying to recall something. "Nah. Same old. Same old. Wait. Wait a sec. There may be this one thing. Then again it may be nothing. When Ellowina was directing, she was always having us adjust the elliptical lights. You know, those smaller spotlights. They had to be just right."

"Go on," Marshall said.

"The night before I found Miranda all laid out, Cliff wanted those lights readjusted. Didn't like Ellowina's setup. What the hell. He's the director now. What did I care? We stayed late and did what he said. Then all of us came here for a quick beer."

"Hmm . . . did Miranda say anything to Cliff? About the lights? Because, from what little I know about theater, it would mean she wasn't going to be in the limelight, God forbid."

"Nope. At least not that I know of. Like I told Phee the other day at the dog park, Miranda was always climbing up that catwalk to readjust the pipe clamps. They're the things that hold the lights. Wouldn't have mattered what Cliff wanted. Miranda was going to get her way."

Wayne gave Bill a nudge and held up his glass. "Well, she got it all right."

It wasn't exactly what I would call a toast, but the men all paused to drink. The conversation continued a while, mostly about Ellowina, Cliff, Miranda, and Sue Ellen before shifting back to Chuck and his inexperience on stage. Herb and his crew decided to stay for another round, but Marshall and I finished our beers.

He said something about having to be up early the next day and tapped my elbow. "Come on, Phee. I'll drive you back to your car."

"Good night, everyone," I said as we left. It wasn't until I got inside Marshall's car and fastened the seatbelt that we were able to continue our conversation.

This way we couldn't be overheard walking through the parking lot.

"Hmm, if I've got this right," Marshall said, "only Randolph and Stanley had actual theater or related experience. Do you have any idea about the others?"

"Not offhand. I could ask my mother. Why?"

"Those guys made an interesting point. The rehearsals have been going on for a few weeks, so you'd think everyone would know their lines by now. Yet Chuck doesn't. Maybe he took care of his real reason for getting into the play and simply needs to bumble through the rest of it so as not to cast suspicion on himself. Just a thought. Like anything else. Still, I'll be doing background checks on all of them."

"I can save you some time as far as my mother's background is concerned."

"Sorry. When I said *all*, I meant Sue Ellen and the male cast members. The ladies in your mother's book club don't even come up on my radar."

"She'll be relieved to hear that. You know, she's been pestering me to have a chat with Stanley, but I've managed to avoid it so far. Do you think he's as volatile as I'm being led to believe? If so, maybe you should drop by the broadcast club. As I recall, they meet at some ungodly hour in the morning."

"Sure. Last thing I'd want is for you to feel uncomfortable, or worse. Heck, you're doing more investigating than us real deals. Sure you're not secretly yearning to trade in those spreadsheets for decent walking shoes and a concealed weapon?"

"Not on your life. And by the way, I do carry a concealed weapon."

I would have bet money his jaw dropped, but it was too dark to tell.

"I carry a—"

Just then a car came screeching into Curley's parking lot and nearly collided with ours. Marshall bolted out of the door before I could finish my sentence. The car, an old Buick, looked familiar. Maybe that was because most of my mother's friends drove an old Buick. I opened the car door, took a step out, and gasped.

It was Shirley, and she really looked as if she had seen a ghost. Or worse yet, another body. Her voice reverberated in the still night air. "Lordy! Lordy! Harriet said you'd be here."

I tried to hide the panic in my voice. "My mother? Is she all right?"

"She's fine. Probably eating another slice of pie at the Homey Hut. I was there too, finishing my cup of coffee, when I realized I left my clutch bag in the costume room. So Cecilia went back with me to get it. We knew the two cleaning ladies would still be there. Oh goodness. Cecilia. I don't know why she's still sitting in the car. Hold on for a second. CECILIA. YOU CAN COME OUT. I DON'T THINK SHE FOLLOWED US."

Marshall took a step toward Shirley's car and opened the passenger door for Cecilia. "Who? Who didn't follow you?"

"Oh Lordy. You're not going to believe me, but it was Miranda's ghost. That's when I called Harriet from the theater, and she said the two of you were going to Curley's to speak with Herb's buddies. Lord All Mighty. I saw it myself. Miranda's ghost."

I could tell Marshall was taken completely off guard. "Um, er, do you think maybe you and Cecilia would want to go inside and sit down?"

"Oh heavens, no. It's bad enough being seen in Curley's parking lot. What do you think, Cecilia?"

By now Cecilia had gotten out of the car and wedged herself between Shirley and Marshall. I didn't think it was possible, but given her dramatic dark attire and lack of makeup, she could have scared someone. The heck with Miranda's ghost. When the parking lot lights illuminated her face, it made her appear more frightening than what I imagined she and Shirley had seen in the theater.

Her voice was loud and direct. "Are the men still in there? If so, I'm not budging. They'll only razz us. I knew we should have taken a picture of it. I kept saying, 'Shirley, take out your phone and snap a picture.'"

"Good Lord. How on earth could I snap a picture when my hands were shaking like leaves in a windstorm? I couldn't even open my clutch to get to the phone. And, speaking of which, you should join the rest of us in the twenty-first century and buy yourself one of those smartphones. No one uses those antiquated flip phones anymore."

Marshall kept turning his head back and forth from Cecilia to Shirley. It was like watching a ping-pong game without having to keep score. "Ladies. Ladies. Can you please backtrack and tell us what happened? What makes you think you saw Miranda's ghost? Start at the beginning."

The expression "start at the beginning" had no reference point for my mother's friends. "The beginning" could refer to the first time Shirley found out about the play or perhaps to the moment she thought Miranda's spirit was haunting the building. I bit my lip and held my breath. Fortunately, as soon as Marshall heard her utter the words "It all started when . . ." he moved up the timeline and saved us the lengthy prologue.

"I didn't want to go alone, and since I drove Cecilia

to rehearsal tonight, she felt she should go with me to the theater. The parking lot was empty, except for the two cars by the maintenance doors. The deputy on duty had already left, so we weren't sure if we could get inside, but the night crew hadn't locked the doors yet, so we walked right in."

Marshall nodded and Shirley continued.

"The hall and foyer lights were still on, so Cecilia and I went down the hallway to the costume room. I have a key, you know. To the costume room. Nothing else. We got inside, and I saw my clutch bag on the counter, I picked it up, and we left the room. We started to go back down the hallway when all of a sudden the lights went out. Cecilia said it was the cleaning ladies turning off everything, but those safety lights in the hall shouldn't have gone off, leaving us in the dark. Lordy, I knew something was wrong. Right there and then. We yelled out for the cleaners, but no one answered. Isn't that right, Cecilia?"

"Oh, yes. Absolutely right. We headed straight for the auditorium because it looked like the wall lights were still on. Then, as soon as we walked in, the lights dimmed and we saw her. It was Miranda all right. On the stage. Wearing one of those shimmery dresses of hers. I would recognize that coiffed hairdo anywhere. She was standing upstage behind the couch. Seemed to come right out of nowhere. I thought my heart was going to jump into my mouth."

Marshall gave Cecilia a quick pat on the shoulder. "Okay, okay. Calm down. What else happened?"

"The lights went off. Not at once. Dimmer and dimmer. Then we were left in the dark. I swear I could feel her breathing on the back of my neck."

"Um," I muttered. "Are you sure that wasn't Shirley? I mean, she was standing right next to you."

"I wasn't breathing down anyone's neck," Shirley said. "In fact, I don't think I was breathing at all. It was awful. Lordy, I couldn't even open my mouth to scream. Not right away. Then the good Lord gave me my voice back, and I screamed. Isn't that right, Cecilia?"

"That's right. We both did. We screamed and screamed our heads off, and then, all of a sudden, wouldn't you know it, but the wall lights came back on in the auditorium, and we could see the safety lights in the hallway."

"Couldn't that woman you saw have been an image from the projector booth?" Marshall asked. "You said she seemed to come out of nowhere. Maybe it was a hologram, and one of the guys from the lighting crew was testing out something."

It was a levelheaded question and something I would have expected to come from Marshall, but Shirley and Cecilia didn't seem to be in a mood for levelheadedness.

I'd never heard Cecilia get so loud. "It could have. It most certainly could have. But it wasn't. It was Miranda all right. And I'll tell you something else. Holograms don't wear perfume. The room was filled with that scent of hers. And as for the lighting crew, those beer-guzzling fancy pants hightailed themselves out of the building as soon as Cliff ended the rehearsal. There was no one there."

"Ladies, there has to be a logical explanation. What about the cleaning crew? You mentioned two women."

"Yes. Yes. They both came running when they heard us scream," Shirley said. "They'd been in the restrooms, and the lights were still on in there. They never knew everything else was pitch black. Said they'd leave it in their nightly report for their supervisor. A lot of help that's going to be."

Marshall let out an audible sigh. "Shirley, did you tell them about the woman you saw?"

"English isn't their native language. Good Lord. We were lucky we could explain about the lights."

Then Cecilia broke in. "I know you're probably wondering why we didn't just drive across the street to the sheriff's posse office, but they wouldn't have believed us. That's when Shirley called Harriet at the Homey Hut and found out where you were."

"I'm surprised my mother didn't announce it to everyone. She was the one who insisted we go to Curley's in the first place to dig for dirt with Herb's crew."

"Get out your shovel, Phee, and start digging," Marshall said. "Looks like the crew is coming this way."

Chapter 16

Sure enough, the entire pinochle playing entourage was headed our way. The traffic from the road behind us was no match for Herb's voice.

"If we knew you were holding a tailgate party, we would've joined you sooner. Hey, Shirley, what brings you and Cecilia here? Don't tell me Miranda's ghost chased you out of the theater."

"Hush! You hush your mouth, Herb Garrett. For your information, Cecilia and I wanted to know how the investigation was going, and Harriet told us Marshall and Phee would be here. We were too busy during rehearsal to talk with them."

"You could have joined us, you know," Bill said. "Ain't like we're going to bite your heads off or anything."

"Maybe another time. And place."

"Okay. Let me know and I'll make reservations at Buckingham Palace for you, or would you prefer the Taj Mahal?"

"What I'd prefer is for—"

Shirley never got to finish her thought. It all happened way too fast. First the bright headlights that blinded all of us, then the rubbery smell from the tires as the car got closer. I expected to hear the screech of brakes like when Shirley had burst into the parking lot, only this driver had no intention of slowing down. The car was headed right toward us.

Marshall shoved the ladies out of the way and screamed at me, "GET OUT OF THE WAY!"

Someone grabbed my arm and yanked me to safety. It was Bill. He and Herb were inches from me while Wayne and Kenny were still a good five or six feet back.

The car never stopped. Whoever was behind the wheel tore across the parking lot and out the other exit. They were back on the road before any of us could catch our breath.

Bill ran to the road in a futile attempt to get a better look at the vehicle. "What the hell? Damn drunks. Did anyone get the license?"

Herb shook his head and gave the parking lot a once-over. "License, my ass. I didn't even see what kind of car it was."

"Lordy, Lordy, I did!" Shirley shrieked. "I saw what kind of car it was. It was Miranda's. Silver and black like the spawn of Satan."

Shirley and Cecilia were literally feeding off each other's panic, and Marshall had all he could do trying to calm them down.

Shirley was insistent Miranda's spirit had put the driver up to this. "It's that she-witch. Back from the grave."

Marshall took Shirley by the arm and spoke softly. "It's not a spirit from beyond. Take it easy. Bill's right. Probably a drunk driver. I'm phoning it in to the sheriff's office. Even without a good description, they can send a car or two down the road and alert the police in Surprise."

As Marshall placed the call, Herb asked Kenny and Wayne if they'd gotten a decent look, but neither of them did.

"If you ask me," Kenny said, "it was kids out drinking and joyriding. Lucky none of us got killed."

"Yet. Yet," Shirley said. "They always come back. You think they're dead, but they always come back. It's that evil spirit Miranda."

Bill stomped his foot and took a step toward Shirley. "What needs to come back are the rational thoughts that have evaporated from your mind."

Kenny made some sort of deep guttural groan and marched directly over to Shirley. "Bill's right. It wasn't a ghost. Ghosts have no way to pay for a license and registration. Not to mention gas."

Cecilia, who had been sniffling and shaking, looked over at Kenny and shouted, "You think that's funny? That's not funny. We weren't going to say anything because we knew you'd make fun of us, but we saw something tonight in the auditorium. Something horrible."

"What? The damn rehearsal schedule for next week?"

"Cecilia's being serious." I glared at Kenny. "She and Shirley saw someone after everyone left the building. They went back inside because they forgot something in the costume room."

Just then Marshall waved his hand and spoke. "I just got off the phone with a sheriff's deputy. They've had reports all night about kids out joyriding. They've got patrol cars on the county roads, and they've notified the Surprise Police Department."

"See," Kenny said as he looked directly at Shirley. "I said it was probably kids out for some kicks."

"Kicks, huh? Maybe if you all stopped talking and

took a deep breath, you might change your mind. Well, go ahead. What do you smell?"

For a minute no one said a word.

Then Bill finally spoke up. "Yeah. Fine. I smell it. Car exhaust. Old cigarette smoke. And, yeah, I hate to say it, but I smell that damn perfume of hers."

"We're in the parking lot that belongs to a local bar. What'd you expect it to smell like?" Kenny asked.

"Not Shalimar," I said. "This isn't the crowd for it, and Curley's isn't the place."

"You recognize the perfume?"

"Unfortunately, yes. It was all the rage when I was a teenager."

Marshall gave me a quick smile and took a step closer to Kenny and Bill. "Look, this isn't getting us anywhere. We're all tired and some of us have work tomorrow. I promise I'll look into the incident in the auditorium. As for the perfume . . . I'm sure we'll figure that out, too. It's certainly been an eventful evening. What do you say we all call it a night and head home?"

Herb and the guys all answered at once.

"No complaints here."

"Yeah, sure."

"I'm beat. Why not?"

"Damn juvenile drivers."

As the guys headed to their cars, Marshall asked Shirley if she was going to be all right driving home. Big mistake. She said no, and insisted Marshall follow her all the way back to her house. Not only that, but since Shirley had given Cecilia a ride to the rehearsal, it meant Marshall had to follow Shirley to Cecilia's house first and then over to Shirley's place before taking me back to my car at the pizza parlor.

What a nightmare. Shirley refused to get behind

the wheel of her car until she was certain no one had snuck in while the commotion was taking place in the parking lot. That meant Marshall had to escort the women to Shirley's car and look under the seats and in the trunk before Shirley was satisfied.

As both women buckled up in the large maroon Buick, Marshall leaned over and spoke to them. "I know what you saw must have been really unnerving, but I think you'll be perfectly safe once you get to your own homes. Phee and I will go inside with you if it'll make you feel any better."

It was worse than tucking in a five-year-old who was scared of the boogieman. Cecilia insisted Marshall check all the closets and the garage. She also wanted him to open her car, which was parked inside, and look on the floor in case something was lurking.

Shirley was worse. Marshall even had to open the dishwasher and look inside the washer and dryer, as well as under the beds. By the time we left her place, we were both wiped out.

"All those teddy bears, Phee. Did you get a look at all those teddy bears?"

We were finally heading out of Sun City West and back to the pizza place.

"Yeah. I've seen the entire collection. Shirley sews them herself. She's amazingly talented."

"Talented and imaginative. I don't know what the heck she and Cecilia saw in that auditorium, but I'll bet anything it came from the projector booth. Maybe someone stayed behind."

"Who? All of the guys were hell-bent on getting out of the rehearsal. You heard that yourself tonight."

"All but one. What if Kevin didn't really go home to be served a hot meal? What if that was a bunch of malarkey to throw us off? He's an electrician and would be more than familiar with projector images."

"But why would he stick around when the rehearsal was over?"

"Good question. Unless he was the one responsible for Miranda's death, and he has another victim in mind."

"Oh my God! That's awful. My mother was right about no one being safe."

"Look, I'm only speculating. Theorizing. That's what we do. I don't have any substantive reason to suspect Kevin of anything. But that's how we investigate. We look at all the inconsistencies and rule them out."

"So, what does that mean?"

"Means I'm going to be doing a little more digging on his background. Somehow, someone other than Len Beckers and Cliff Edwards had relationships with Miranda Lee."

"You don't think Kevin dated her, too? Before he was married, I mean. Because if he did, I'm positive Herb would blab that all around."

"I don't know about dating her, but there are lots of reasons outside of the intimate ones that might lead to murder. Like I said before, I need to find out if there are any connections Miranda might have had in her past that resulted in her death."

"What bothers me, Marshall, is the fact all this weird stuff seems to be going on in the theater. Let's face it, everyone knows Shirley and Cecilia believe in the afterlife. Ghosts, if you will. So, it could be quite possible Miranda's killer is trying to throw us off by creating this hubbub and using them as the perfect patsies. Geez, I wish this play would be over with."

"When's opening night? I know it's coming up soon."

"The first week in December. On a Friday night. The play will run that weekend and the next."

"The first week in December? That's only two weeks away, more or less."

"I know. Not much rehearsal time left. Plus, they won't be practicing on Thanksgiving Day or Black Friday. According to my mother, if they called a rehearsal for the Friday after Thanksgiving, they'd be missing half the cast and most of the crew."

Marshall laughed as he turned into the pizza parlor's lot. I was surprised the place wasn't deserted. In fact, it seemed even more crowded than it was a few hours before.

"My gosh. I'm glad we ate when we did. We'd never get a seat now. I keep forgetting this is 'the real world' and not Sun City West, where everything closes at eight."

"Looks like your car is still in one piece. You going to be okay getting home, or did you want me to follow you? It's no bother. Really."

My God! What's he going to do now? Offer to check inside the closets and under the bed?

"I'll be fine. If Miranda's ghost follows me home, I'll share a nightcap with her."

"I can think of better company."

Is that a proposal? A proposition? A what? "You can say that again. Well, I'd better get going, or I might as well just drive straight into work. Thanks, Marshall. You were a good sport to put up with Shirley and Cecilia."

"It was kind of fun, actually. Except for those teddy bears. I'm going to have nightmares about finding them under my bed."

"I think you'll be safe. See you in the morning."

Marshall waited while I started my car and drove out of the lot. I was so damn tempted to invite him back to my place, but then what? I was too old to be playing the damsel in distress. Besides, he'd see right through me. Maybe Shirley and Cecilia were freaked out about spirits, but Marshall knew me better. If anything was going to develop between the two of us, it would have to take a different course.

Chapter 17

It was way too late to give my mother a call when I got in, so the following morning I sent her a quick email. Essentially, I postponed the inevitable conversation we would have regarding any gossip Marshall and I managed to glean from Herb and the lighting crew.

Augusta was already at her desk when I walked into our office. "Good morning, Phee. Mr. Williams is in his office and said I should send you right in as soon as I saw you."

"Thanks, Augusta. I can barely keep my eyes open. You wouldn't believe the night I had, thanks to my mother's play."

"Mr. Gregory didn't sound so good, either. He left a message. Something about going to a radio station."

"Stanley Krumpmeyer."

"What? Who's that?"

"That's the person Marshall's going to see. Possibly a suspect. Oh, what the heck. Everyone in that play is a suspect. I'll tell you about it when I get a chance. I'd better go see what Nate wants."

"Oh. One more thing. Your mother called."

"Aargh. Did she leave a message?"

"I'm pretty good about taking messages, Phee. I've been doing this for a long time. Truth be told, all I understood was for you to call her and something about a dead woman haunting your mother's friends. Is this the same dead woman from the catwalk?"

"Yes and no. Some of my mom's friends who are on the crew insist they've seen Miranda Lee's ghost. That was the victim. Miranda Lee. As for the ghost . . . I don't know what to tell you. Anyway, I don't want to keep Nate waiting."

"Sure thing, Phee."

I gave a quick knock on the door and let myself into Nate's office.

He was sitting at his computer, cup of coffee in hand. "Hey, kiddo! Heard you had a fun night. Marshall sent me a text."

"If by fun you mean watching someone check under beds and in closets for ghosts or boogiemen, then I'd say I had a fabulous night. Honestly, Nate, my mother's friends are unbelievable. I can't possibly imagine what's going through Marshall's head right now."

"I wouldn't worry about it if I were you. Listen, you and Marshall can thank me later, but I've got something for you." Nate reached across his desk and handed me a manila envelope.

"What's this?"

"A four-year-old lawsuit that never came to fruition."

"Huh?"

"When I started to do a background check on Miranda Lee, I found this little tidbit of information. It may not amount to much, but then again, I've seen weaker motives for murder."

"What is it?" My hands were working frantically to open the envelope and see for myself.

Meanwhile, Nate jumped ahead. "Miranda was suing the local purebred kennel club and its board for refusing to list her dog, Lady Lee, as a purebred Chinese Crested Hairless, whatever the heck those are. But take a good look at who was listed on the kennel club board at the time."

"Oh my gosh. Gordon Web. The guy who plays Giles Ralston in the play. Cindy Dolton from the dog park told me he owns a Pomeranian. But that's not all. Gordon was the one who nearly broke a leg falling through an open trapdoor on the stage. You don't suppose he did that to himself to throw everyone off? Maybe he killed her."

"Like I said, it's a weak motive, but there may be more to it. I've got to head back to Tucson in less than an hour, so when Marshall gets back, show him this and see what he thinks. The other information on Miranda is also in there."

"Soon as I take a break, I'll look it over."

"Who are you kidding, Phee? You won't be able to leave that envelope alone for more than ten seconds. Go on. I know you'll get the accounting done."

"You know me too well. Have a good drive to Tucson." I rushed into my office, booted up my computer and plopped myself in front of my desk. I felt like a ten-year-old kid who'd ditched school to read comic books in the john, but instead of reading about Archie and Veronica, I was prying into Miranda's life and savoring every last detail.

The envelope contained computerized records, a few handwritten notes (from Nate presumably), and some photocopies from various places of employment.

Paula Darren was right. According to verification of employment, Miranda had been a registered nurse at the Brookridge Rehabilitation Center in Phoenix. It was one of a long series of nursing positions she'd held since first starting out in her home state of Rhode Island. I thought Paula had mentioned that, too. Something about cremation and a niece being the only living relative. But the mention of Rhode Island plagued me. Where had I heard it before in reference to the play?

Systematically, I went through each of the cast members and tried to remember what I'd heard about them. Finally, it dawned on me, but it wasn't specific. Something Myrna had told my mother about Randolph Tilden Jr. being a retired theater professor from back east, possibly Rhode Island.

I jumped out of my seat and headed back to Nate's office. Did he or Marshall do a background check on Randolph?

"If you're looking for Mr. Williams, he left a few minutes ago."

"Drat. Thanks, Augusta."

"Anything I can get for you?"

"I don't think so. I was hoping Nate or Marshall had done a background check on one of the cast members."

"Can't help you with that, but Marshall should be in any minute."

"Okay."

I walked back to my desk and tried to remember what else I'd heard about Randolph. Midway through a spreadsheet update, I recalled the conversation I'd had with Louise. She, too, knew Randolph had prior theater experience, but there was something else. A feeling Louise had, and it wasn't a good one. If Randolph was the type who was capable of "tearing the wings off of flies," would he also be the type to commit murder? Especially if his path and Miranda's crossed way back in Rhode Island.

I had to get that background information on Randolph or I wouldn't be able to concentrate on anything. Poor Marshall. The minute I heard him say hello to Augusta, I was out of my office and standing directly in front of him. He couldn't make a move without bumping into me.

"Hey, Phee. Get any sleep last night?"

"Do I look that bad?"

"Uh, no. Just asking because I had barely closed my eyes when the alarm went off. Your mother's friends are quite the trip."

"Yeah. Um. Sorry about that."

"Like I said last night, it was kind of amusing. Certainly more amusing than the conversation I had with Stanley Krumpmeyer first thing this morning. Boy, what a jerk! Forget about rage being a motive for him killing Miranda. Seems to me the guy gets off on arguing. Said his verbal altercations with her kept his mind sharp and focused. Was sorry he lost a sparring partner. Can you imagine? And as far as information goes, all he gave me was a rehash of what we already knew. Nothing useful."

"I may have something useful. I mean, I need to find something out that might be useful. Did you or Nate conduct a background check on Randolph? He's the one who supposedly had an earache the day Miranda's body was found."

"Not yet. At least I didn't, and if Nate did, then he would have shared it with me. Don't look so distressed. I can get going on it right away. Why is it so important?"

"I think there might have been a connection between him and Miranda. But only if he taught in some college in Rhode Island. If that state doesn't show up, don't waste your time with the rest."

"Fair enough. I think we can rule out Stanley as a suspect, but let me see about churning up something on our infamous Mr. Tilden before my first appointment arrives."

"Thanks, Marshall. Really."

He shrugged and smiled at the same time before turning toward his office.

"Psst!" Augusta motioned for me to move in closer to her desk.

"I'm telling you, Phee," she said once Marshall was out of earshot, "he likes you."

My face warmed. "That may change once he gets a closer look at the family tree. By the way, are you calling out for lunch?"

"I was thinking about it. Why?"

"I've got so much to catch up on and don't feel like leaving the office."

"Then it's settled. Pizza or deli? Let me know."

I thanked her and trotted back to my desk, where I spent the next forty-five minutes going over some bills. I heard Augusta speaking with Marshall's first appointment of the day and knew I'd have to wait until he found the time to complete that background check on Randolph.

At a little past eleven, I informed Augusta I'd be fine with a ham and Swiss on rye or any kind of pizza. Her choice.

"You must be sick of pizza, Phee. Let's order deli sandwiches."

As she picked up the phone to place our orders, Marshall stepped out of his office.

"Oh good, Phee. You're here. Well, for your information, Randolph taught theater in Massachusetts.

Boston to be precise. Emerson College to be even more specific."

"Darn it. It was such a possibility."

"Don't look so downtrodden. I uncovered another little morsel that might just lead to something. Guess who else is from Rhode Island?"

Augusta slapped some papers on her desk and leaned in to listen.

I could barely contain myself. "Who? Who? Not Gordon? Not Chuck? Kevin? Was it Kevin? You're not about to make me go through the entire cast and crew are you?"

"Do I look like the kind of person who would do a thing like that?"

Augusta picked up the papers she had stacked and thrust them down again on her desk. This time harder. "I don't have all day. I need to place our lunch orders. Who is it?"

Marshall jumped back with a wide grin. "Whoa, Augusta. This detective business must be rubbing off on you."

"Only the drama Phee brings in. Make it snappy and tell us who it is."

He let out a quick laugh along with three words— "Sue Ellen Blair."

I was dumbfounded. "What? Sue Ellen Blair? Sweet little Sue Ellen from Wisconsin? I thought she told everyone she moved here from Wisconsin."

Augusta chuckled and shook her head. "She probably did. Maybe she got sick of the east coast and had a hankering for cheese. Or maybe she committed some horrific heinous crime in Rhode Island and moved to a state where no one would think to look."

"You know what I think?" Marshall asked. "I think you should be writing crime novels."

"Right now, the only thing I'm going to be writing is our order for the deli so I get it right when I call. Now, if you two will excuse me, I'd better start dialing."

Marshall and I stepped away from Augusta's desk until we were leaning against the copier. I was so frazzled by Marshall's revelation, I just stood there with my mouth wide open. Finally, a few words spewed out. It would take a seasoned detective or perhaps a linguist to decipher those words, but Marshall took a crack at it anyway.

"If you're asking if Miranda and Sue Ellen lived in the same city, I don't know. Not yet. Only got as far as birth certificates. Miranda was what? In her early sixties? Sue Ellen looks to be a late baby boomer, fifties at most. Still, their paths could have crossed."

"Oh my gosh, Marshall. I was so caught up with my own theories I forgot to give you some information Nate turned up. It's about Gordon Web and a lawsuit regarding Miranda's Chinese Crested Hairless."

"Her what?"

"Dog. A pedigree dog. Or in this case, maybe not. The Sun City West Purebred Kennel Club, of which Gordon was on the board, refused to recognize Miranda's dog, and she filed a lawsuit. Um, the dog died a few years ago, and the lawsuit never came to fruition, but maybe Gordon harbored a grudge."

"Oh brother. Working this case is like trying to stick a fork into spaghetti to pull out a strand. I'll see what else I can turn up on Sue Ellen for starters and—"

"Believe it or not, people are beginning to recognize me at the dog park. As much as I hate running the risk of having one of those ankle biters pee on my leg, I think I'll drop by after work and see what I can find out about Gordon and Miranda. I'll keep my fingers crossed no one at the park tells my mother I went without taking Streetman. He's exhaustive, and I need to talk with Cindy Dolton. Last I knew from her, Gordon and Miranda kept a wide berth from each other. Maybe someone else knows something."

"Check that list of kennel club board members again and see if anything pops out at you. And if you do decide to go to that park, I wouldn't wear open-toed shoes."

"Eeew. Maybe I'll go tomorrow after work, and, in the meantime, I'll see if my mom or her friends recognize any of the names on the list."

"Good idea. I'll delve deeper into any Rhode Island connections. Anyway, I've got a few things to finish up before I head out to lunch with a, um . . . client. Enjoy your deli takeout."

Lunch? Client? Why the pause before "client?" Is that a nice way of him saying he has a date?

Marshall turned and went back to his office while I stood at the copier with a blank look on my face.

"Everything okay?" Augusta asked.

"Oh, yeah. Sure."

"The food will be here in twenty minutes."

Suddenly I didn't feel like eating. All I could think of was Marshall's lunch date. If it was a date.

I walked over to Augusta and whispered, "Do you know who he's having lunch with?"

Augusta grabbed the mouse and changed screens. "He didn't say?"

"No. And . . . uh . . . I was wondering . . ."

"Well, you have nothing to worry about. And you didn't hear it from me. He's meeting the deacon from St. Mark's Episcopal Church. Say, didn't I read in the paper about some thefts of artwork there? That must be what the meeting is about."

Augusta quickly shifted to another screen. "So, as I was saying, lunch should be here shortly."

"That's terrific! I'm famished."